The Questions
Retro Edition

By the same authors

The Questions – Classic Edition
ISBN 1-904999-09-3

The Questions - First Compendium Edition
ISBN 1-904999-11-5

The Questions
Retro Edition

Fiona McCade
William O'Leary
Cath Sutton

K&B
Kennedy & Boyd

Published by
Kennedy and Boyd
an imprint of
Zeticula
57 St Vincent Crescent
Glasgow
G3 8NQ

http://www.kennedyandboyd.co.uk
admin@kennedyandboyd.co.uk

First published in 2004

ISBN 1-904999-10-7 Paperback

http://www.thequestions.co.uk

The Retro Questions are dedicated to the glory of all strong opinions,
however petty or ill-informed they may be

Acknowledgements

Cath, Fiona and William would like to thank all these lovely people for their invaluable help, their forthright opinions and their unfailing commitment to trivia: Libby Bell, Marcus Berkmann, Matthew Brander, Donald Brown, James Costain, A.J Cotter, Dylan Dowd, Petula Dowe, Ceri Essex, Jes Fernie, Kirsty Fulford, John Gore, Iain Harper, Stuart Johnston, Jennifer Jones, Peter Jones, Paul Kent, Andrew Leith, James Leslie, John Macgill, Chris Maguire, Ian Marr, James McCade, Shirley McCade, Roy McMillan, Patricia 'Dandelion and Burdock' Miller, Robert and Helen Miller, Heather Montgomery, Richard Phillips, Maria Quinn, Anna Redfern, Elisabeth Reissner, Jeanne Saint, George Sutton, Vivian Sutton, Wal Sutton, Janet de Vigne, Abigail Youngman.

Introduction

One of your first Questions was probably "Mum or Dad?", based on the dilemma of which one would best understand your basic, human need to own a pair of Clackers and give you the money to buy them. Growing up in the Western world meant that our childhoods were spent making many choices like this one. We fought in the playground over whose toy was better than whose, then we graduated to arguing over which sweet tasted best, which TV show was coolest, which book, which film, which band, and so on, until we had created ourselves out of a mass of tiny predilections, most of which still hold as true today as they did when Ritchie Cunningham had hair.

As we grew up, so did popular culture. Like Dr Who, the Questions are constantly metamorphosing and we've exhumed some long-forgotten incarnations for you to revisit and get really annoyed about all over again. For instance, although the "Oasis or Blur?" Question hasn't been asked since 1997, we've preserved it here, should you and your mates ever need something to argue about next time you're stuck in Anchorage during an air-traffic controllers' strike.

The rules are simple. Each Question offers an either/or choice. All you need to find out is which of the two alternatives your subject prefers. That's it. Obviously, the only right answer is the one that pleases you, but whatever reply you receive will tell you plenty about the person responding and, most importantly, whether or not you can bear to spend another moment in their company. To help you get into the mood, and as a guide to using the method, we've included our humble opinions on each Question.

The Questions are a great way to meet people, because they guarantee that you'll never again be without an opening conversational gambit. To begin any new relationship, simply:

1) Approach your subject.
2) Light the touch paper of conversation with a well-chosen Question.
3) Wait for the sparks to fly.
4) If conversation fails to ignite, withdraw and only return to throw cold water over the ungrateful sod. They don't deserve you.

The Retro Questions deal with the really big issues; the things most fundamental to a well-lived life, like cartoons, desserts and fanciable people. They cover a broad spectrum of trivia, so unless you're an Amish lighthouse keeper, there will be something in here to rekindle the passionately held beliefs of your formative years. The most important thing is simply to have an opinion. Whining that something was before - or even after - your time is no excuse. A little research goes a long way and the Retro Questions can help you impress someone much older - or younger - than you. It's a great way to date someone, in both meanings of the word.

Occasionally, re-visiting sensitive childhood memories can be traumatic, so keep some Kleenex handy in case of nostalgia-emergencies. Likewise, imposing unnecessary conditions on any Question is potentially dangerous. In one regrettable instance, a subject wilfully turned a harmless "Piglet or Pooh?" query into a sort of Sophie's Choice, became extremely emotional and broke down. (The key is *not* to imagine you are leaving one of them behind with the Nazis, although if you insist, we suggest taking Pooh, as Piglet could probably escape more easily, being smaller and less noticeable.)

The Dalai Lama says "I think it is foolish to create a quarrel on a basis of 'I like this' and 'you like that'." And he's quite right. Very foolish, but great fun. Ask any Question of the right person and you'll either take up arms, or fall into each other's arms. Either way, play nicely together and if you feel you simply can't bear to stay friends with someone who still insists that Coe was superior to Ovett, take a very deep breath and forgive them. They know not what they do.

Besides, harmony isn't always what we're looking for. Opposites attract; conflict guarantees drama – and maybe even passion. You can use the Questions to explore your dark side and seek out someone who fits in with your deepest, most shameful desires. Are you a good, *Blue Peter* girl who secretly hankers after a bit of *Magpie* rough? This is how to find him.

Here we go.

Which do you prefer?

The Questions

Question 1

ABBA:
Agnetha or Annifrid?

AGNETHA: Abba is essentially a Viking saga of how a round, hairy troll and his tiny pixie friend managed to snare two lovely Scandinavian sirens and went on to conquer the world together. This happened at the same time as I was starting to feel the first stirrings of manhood. Whenever I imagined myself as a Viking warrior (a symptom of the stirrings), returning home from raping and pillaging, who was waiting for me, with a wild boar on the spit and a stein of mead? Agnetha. She was my mental template for a Viking woman – blonde, blue-eyed and buxom.

Now I look at this question as an adult, with slightly more sophisticated considerations, I admit Annifrid might have edged it, but I can't ignore the terrible perm incident of 1974-75. Even if I could have overlooked this, she repeated the mistake in 1980, but this time with plum highlights. The Viking warrior in me demands I choose Agnetha, and I can find no reason to disagree. **WOL**

ANNIFRID: Oh, ye of little taste. You just can't see past the peroxide, can you? My God, if I hear Agnetha trilling on about how lucky she is to have all that golden hair one more time, I'll buy a Buck's Fizz record. I mean it. Even Frida's own group were against her - making her sing backing vocals to Goldilocks, when she was so obviously much lovelier to look at and had more talent in her pinkie nail than Agnetha 'Rear of the Year' Faltskog had in her entire existence. Somehow, possibly thanks to a couple of dodgy hair-dos (even I can't defend the Waterloo perm), Frida never seemed to get as much attention as Miss Blue Eye Shadow 1977, despite having superior bone structure and a far lovelier voice. Open your eyes, world. Watch the *Fernando* video and worship at the feet of the Norwegian Nightingale. **FM**

Question 2

Starsky or Hutch?

STARSKY: Funnier, sexier, cooler, darker; not forgetting the car, the car and oh, the car. I don't want to knock Ken – absolute respect for the obviously distressing car-roof incident in the credits – but you can't beat Dave. He's not a pretty boy. He's got grit, he's got oomph and he fills his jeans so well. Most importantly, you can really believe he's a tough guy, rather than someone who just walked out of a shop window. Ah, but I can't get nasty. Starsky's the man, but in the end, they're two guys who love each other, who just happen to be cops. **FM**

HUTCH: He is the feng to Starsky's shui. You needed both to create the magic, but I have to pick one, so Hutch it is. I was very young when I formulated my preference, but even then I knew I wanted my plain-clothes cops lucid, gentle and laid back. I couldn't be doing with Starsky's tense, I-get-my-panties-in-a-wad-at-every-opportunity attitude. Hutch had better hair, didn't have bandy legs and anyone who can land on top of a car in such spectacular style, and still keep moving, deserves my lifelong admiration. **CS**

Question 3

Top puddings: Angel Delight or Arctic Roll?

ANGEL DELIGHT: Ever since the fifth century BC, when the Greek physician Hippocrates first discovered butterscotch, the goal of Western science was to find a way of turning it into a lightly whipped pudding. In 1273, Pope Blessed Gregory X declared that it was heresy to even mention the possibility of such a lightly whipped pudding, which is why it wasn't until the nineteenth century that one man, Alfred Bird, was brave enough to begin the quest again.

Although Alfred himself never stumbled across the magic formula, years later, in 1967, his company did. From then on, it became one of the essential food groups for children, and it is still the best way of ensuring kids get their recommended daily dose of propane-1 and disodium phosphate.

It comes in a range of flavours, but chocolate, banana and butterscotch are the best. Be careful not to overdose on it though. Fairport Convention did and wrote a song (*Angel Delight*) whilst under the influence. It includes references to a peacock avoiding concrete fairies. I bet they'd had too much of the lime flavour. **WOL**

ARCTIC ROLL: The best thing in the world, bar none. It was only wheeled out on special occasions and boy, was it special. The magical triumvirate of ice cream, sponge and jam was a gift from the gods. The ice cream used in an Arctic Roll tasted like no other on this earth and cannot be replicated as a single entity. If eaten from the inside out, the delectable middle melted into the sponge and jam, giving the outer circumference a perfectly moist texture and creating, if you will, the pudding Nirvana.

Angel Delight is a mousse and mousses aren't desserts, but a heinous crime committed against the unwary; they should be put into a capsule and fired into space. Arctic Rolls should be worshipped. **CS**

Question 4

Blue Peter or Magpie?

BLUE PETER: *Blue Peter* has always been the rock upon which British youth can depend. Even though, every Christmas, millions of us ran screaming as our Advent Crowns went up in flames, we knew *Blue Peter* had our best interests at heart. And should we happen to find ourselves drowning, we could be confident that the *Blue Peter* lifeboat was on its way to save us.

You can always rely upon a *Blue Peter* kid because, thanks to this beloved programme, they know everything – from the life-story of Isambard Kingdom Brunel, to the best way of making an Exocet missile out of upturned egg cartons, Fairy Liquid bottles and sticky-back you-know-what.

No *Magpie* watcher will ever rule the world. They were the sort of kids that called their parents by their first names and had their jewellery confiscated. My best friend, Helen Williamson, summed it up perfectly when she sneered: "You know the *Magpie* Christmas Appeal? They ask for *money*." And I think we know who really vandalised the *Blue Peter* garden, don't we? **FM**

MAGPIE: I was actually a *Blue Peter* viewer, it must be said, but I would want any prospective amour or friend to have preferred *Magpie*. Oh God, yes. So much more hip and cool. You knew a *Magpie* man would be behind the bike sheds breaking all the rules, while the *Blue Peter* viewers were simply collecting their bikes.

Magpie was on ITV, which in itself was enough to lend it an air of the illicit, because nice girls didn't watch anything but the BBC. The *Magpie* presenters were jeans-wearing, bra-less hippies and Mick looked just like Marc Bolan. They discussed pop music in depth and were watched by people who would grow up to have a lot more fun. **CS**

Question 5

Charlie's Angels: Kate Jackson or Farrah Fawcett?

KATE JACKSON: A fine feminist icon if ever there was one. She was feisty, bright and didn't have a ludicrous amount of bleach-blonde hair. Sabrina was the courageous one; the Angel we all wanted to be in the playground. Fawcett's Jill was purely decorative and there was no attempt to try and make us believe she was a serious private detective. The only purpose she served was as a reminder to floss.
I tried this Question out at a dinner party and all the women present agreed that if a man they were contemplating dating picked Fawcett over Jackson, it was over before it had even begun. **CS**

FARRAH FAWCETT: I agree. With all that hair and all those teeth (how do Americans get so many teeth into one mouth?), Fawcett was like a cartoon; a spoof Barbie; a scary, carnival freak-show version of Miss America. No red-blooded, right-thinking man with a choice of the original Angels would go for anyone other than Jaclyn Smith, but as she's not an option here (we're obviously examining the extremes), I will go for Farrah. Why? Because one morning I would wake up to find she had turned into Cheryl Ladd. **WOL**

Question 6

Beano or Dandy?

BEANO: People always say "*Beano* and *Dandy*", don't they? Never the other way round. Somehow, the *Beano* always comes first and rightly too, because it's better.

The *Beano* has Dennis the Menace and Gnasher. Frankly, Gnasher alone is enough to bring me on side, but throw in the Bash Street Kids, Billy Whizz and Lord Snooty (who once beat off the Nazi threat with the help of Napoleon - always a recommendation as far as I'm concerned) and I'm with the *Beano* all the way.

But the most historically significant figure in the *Beano* is Minnie the Minx, the greatest proto-feminist of the last century. Move aside Emmeline Pankhurst, Minnie even kicked Dennis the Menace's arse. She inspired generations of girls to grow up into strong, jumper-wearing women who weren't afraid of a scrap. Originally conceived as an Amazon warrior, she never disappointed her disciples. Compared to Minnie, the *Dandy's* Beryl the Peril was just Olive Oyl with PMT. **FM**

DANDY: Bully Beef, Peter's Pocket Grandpa and Spunky and his Spider all enriched my childhood long before I knew what a double-entendre was. Yet it's a single icon that wins this question for the longest running comic in the world. Yep, the king of all comic-book characters has to be the *Dandy's* very own Desperate Dan.

I loved Desperate Dan. He looked like my dad, ate whole cow pies, and smoked a pipe made from a dustbin and old iron drainpipe. Then in 1997 he struck oil, became a millionaire and ran away with the Spice Girls. So, I wrote to DC Thomson suggesting they replace Dan with a more contemporary strip called Desperate DNA, revealing the japes and scrapes of a super-powerful, double-stranded macromolecule. I even suggested a by-line: 'Maybe it don't bend lampposts, but it's got two polynucleotide chains and it's held together by weak thermodynamic forces'. They never replied.

Meanwhile, a worldwide campaign forced Desperate Dan out of retirement and there's now a statue of him in his hometown of Dundee. It's the best thing about Dundee. **WOL**

Question 7

Lennon or McCartney?

LENNON: Musically, Lennon was the Snakebite and McCartney the 'black'. Together, they make a great combination, but you'd retch if you had to have the blackcurrant on its own. Although that might just be me.

When they hit our consciousness, John was the witty one and Paul the pretty one. John was an intelligent, working-class rebel, and he made it cool to be Scouse (no mean achievement in itself). His rebelliousness may have been unfocused and inconsistent at times, but he knew he could use his personality and fame to draw attention to the big issues he felt passionately about - and at least he tried.

It was a tragedy that Lennon's life ended when it did, but it's been equally tragic to see Paul develop a bizarre need to hang around with cartoons and fictional characters, like Rupert Bear, Michael Jackson and Heather Mills. Also, despite any inconsistencies Lennon may have had, I am quite sure that if he were alive today, we wouldn't be referring to him as Sir John. **WOL**

McCARTNEY: I love them both deeply and equally, but John doesn't need me and Paul does. Since December 8th 1980, John has been unable to do any wrong, but Paul has. It's called being alive. So it's the duty of Beatles fans everywhere to support Paul and defend him against those who would praise John to Paul's undeserving detriment.

This is a heartbreaking dilemma for me. I can't separate them musically - I hum the *Frog Chorus* daily - so I think the bottom line is that Paul just pips John at the post in the domesticity stakes. Can you honestly think of a more perfect husband and father? Given the choice of running off into the sunset with one of them, I'd have to choose Paul, because I could rely on him to create domestic bliss. I know John could bake a mean loaf, but I suspect that if I needed someone to stride across windswept moors to repair a fence, Paul would get out there and do it, while John would sneak back to bed. And he's so very lovely. God made Paul, then rested; his work was done. **FM**

Question 8

Scooby-Doo or
Hong Kong Phooey?

SCOOBY-DOO: Daphne. The first cartoon girl I ever fancied and far more attractive than most non-cartoon girls. God, how I used to wish I was a cartoon boy. I'd fantasise about consoling her, once the cocksure Fred finally took a wrong turn in the abandoned theme-park, or old motel. Daphne is the logical conclusion of man learning to draw. What would she look like in a nurse's uniform? What would she look like first thing in the morning? Why didn't I learn to draw, so I could find out? **WOL**

HONG KONG PHOOEY: The mild-mannered janitor wins hands down. He and the clever, faithful Spot (the Holmes to Phooey's Watson) were the ultimate, crime-fighting duo. His incompetence and Spot's world-weary brilliance were irresistible. We had the Phooeymobile; we had the Hong Kong Book of Kung Foo (consulted at times of stress); we had a far better time than we did watching a bunch of pesky, drug-addled teenagers hunting bad-tempered men in sheets. *Hong Kong Phooey* had panache, humour and a groovy, groovy style – something that fans of *Scooby-Doo* quite clearly lacked. **CS**

Question 9

The Jacksons or
the Osmonds?

THE JACKSONS: The Osmonds were all horrible white suits and scary teeth. They certainly didn't produce anything like the sweet sounds of the Jacksons, whose songs made you want to shift your feet to the beat. The only reason the Osmonds are ever given an airing is for their kitsch value, or perhaps because people want to know what a singing Mormon sounds like. The Jacksons, with hair bigger than many small republics, were always cool and produced some awesome pop melodies. Whatever strange goings-on have occurred since the Jacksons' heyday, they're still the ones that make you feel like dancing. **CS**

THE OSMONDS: Who wants to be cool? Sometimes, it's just fun to watch a bunch of Mormons trying to look like Elvis in Las Vegas and singing about crayzee horses. Weeeow! Weeeow!

The Osmonds are all still around, being cute, raising cute families and not dangling them out of windows. None of them have paid surgeons to make them into a cross between Diana Ross and Elizabeth Taylor. None of them have been accused of molesting anybody. Everything's fine in Osmondworld. They made a nice noise, they made people happy and they have lived to thoroughly enjoy it.

The Jacksons may seem more hip, but when do you ever hear them played these days – outside of exercise classes, that is? **FM**

Question 10

Pictionary or
Trivial Pursuit?

PICTIONARY: So much more fun. All Trivial Pursuit does is give the floor to those who labour under the false impression that they're intelligent. No, no, no! They just have good memories for useless information and what's the point of that, unless you want to win at a rubbish board game? Pictionary is for those of us who enjoy playing in a team, have an imagination, and aren't smart arses. **CS**

TRIVIAL PURSUIT: Why do I choose Trivial Pursuit? This is why:
Trivs: "Blue. Geography." *"Great, I'm good at geography."* "OK. Of which country is the Bolivar the currency?" *"Er, Bolivia?"* "No, Venezuela!" *"Bugger, I thought it might be a trick question."* "Yeah. Anyway, my go."
Pictionary: "Skateboard?" *"What do you mean, skateboard? It's an otter!"* "How is that an otter? Where are the forepaws?" *"There!" (Pointing furiously.)* "How are those forepaws? They look round, like little wheels...and there are the axles...and the rest is the deck." *"What the **** are you on about? It's an otter. Have you ever seen a ****ing otter, you moron?"* "Yes, but I've also seen a skateboard and that looks more like a skateboard. I'm just saying, if you wanted me to say 'otter' you should have drawn something that looks like a bloody otter." *"You can play by yourself then, you t**t, and don't think you're sleeping with me tonight, either."* **WOL**

Question 11

Dallas or Dynasty?

DALLAS: *Dynasty* was fine, but it only existed because *Dallas* - the first, and forever the best, of the US super-soaps - had been such a huge hit. Everybody remembers where they were when JR was shot (easy, in front of the telly), because the nation was united in *Dallas* fever. *Dynasty* never had the same impact, because it was more of the same, except in chilly Colorado rather than steamy Texas and there were no Oil Barons' balls.

The characters in *Dynasty* were too icy and elegant for me, and even Krystle's bizarre Princess Di impersonation didn't liven things up. The Carringtons had been rich too long, whereas the Ewings were still red in tooth and claw, first-generation hustlers. (But in the "Ewing or Barnes?" Question, I was with Cliff.)

Jock may have been the daddy of the Ewings, but *Dallas* was the daddy of all soaps. I loved it dearly and wish it had never ended. Unless…maybe it didn't end? Maybe that was all just a dream? **FM**

DYNASTY: Bigger shoulder pads; bigger hair; Joan Collins. *Dynasty* was the most perfect expression of Eighties greed, excess and tastelessness, and it positively revelled in it. It also had a self-awareness and humour that *Dallas* just didn't have. It wasn't filled with annoying Texan accents, enormous Stetsons or Miss Ellie (the one they should have shot). We had a character called Caress; we had not only the voice, but also the body of Charlie from *Charlie's Angels*; we even had a guest appearance by Henry Kissinger. We had a winner. **CS**

Question 12

The Professionals:
Bodie or Doyle?

BODIE: Bodie is the man; the man with the haircut, the car, the leather jackets and the hunky polo-necks. He was the tough guy, the ex-mercenary and Para. He could have taken ol' bubble-headed Ray 'I like to paint' Doyle with both hands tied around a blonde. Who could prefer a Leo Sayer look-alike to Action Man in the flesh? Bodie was the real deal hero, who single-handedly made the Ford Capri a style icon while Doyle was prevaricating between a TR7 and an Escort. Bodie was macho, cute as hell, and quite obviously, a very, very naughty boy. **FM**

DOYLE: Doyle didn't look like a puzzled gorilla, was able to act and didn't pout in an annoying way. He was the hippy, the one that took the ginseng and wore the jeans. He also had the sense not to go for those strange, not to mention vile, polyester-trouser and polo-neck jumper combos that made Bodie look like the Man at C&A. He didn't feel the need to beat everybody to a pulp, could string a sentence together, and had a very nice bottom. **CS**

Question 13

Rod Hull and Emu or Keith Harris and Orville?

ROD HULL AND EMU: The combination of Rod Hull and his grotesque, testy and offensive puppet was utterly hilarious, anarchic and unequalled. Rod Hull gave Emu a whole personality and such was his success, you completely believed that the bird existed as a separate entity. Together they created chaos and mayhem, and I loved every second. The way Emu curled his beak with disgust, or turned to stare at the audience to convey his scorn for the proceedings, made me laugh out loud - and very few things do that. I loved his anger and total disrespect for celebrity, like when he attacked the Queen Mother's bouquet, or rolled Parky around on the floor. Not something the horrible green duck in a nappy was wont to do.

I told myself I mustn't be too rude about Keith Harris and his vile, singing bird, so I have to stop now. **CS**

KEITH HARRIS AND ORVILLE: Rod Hull was a lousy ventriloquist. **FM**

Question 14

The Sex Pistols or
The Clash?

THE SEX PISTOLS: They never pretended to be anything other than well-marketed exhibitionists, but their volume and venom were real. As far as I was concerned, their impact was beyond incredible, because they were the manifestation of all the rebellious thoughts I'd ever harboured. Loud, obnoxious and uncaring - they were everything I could never be and still get invited to parties. Played loud and played often, the Pistols were my scream of hatred at the world. They allowed a young, Surrey girl to get in touch with her darker side and this is my opportunity to thank them. **CS**

THE CLASH: The Clash were one of many bands inspired to join the punk movement by the Sex Pistols, but they not only proved to be better than their muse, they were also better than most other second-wave punk bands. Their brand of youthful dissent was more musically intelligent and politically astute than the Pistols'. They had a clear, revolutionary-socialist message and they could even play their instruments properly.

The Sex Pistols, on the other hand, were never really about music (though the only album they ever produced was pretty darn good), nor were they really about politics. Nihilism and anarchy were to them what T-shirts saying 'Sharon's Hen Party' are to gaggles of drunken and debauched girls - convenient labels to justify their behaviour.

No, the Sex Pistols were essentially something very un-punk indeed – a promotional gimmick for Malcolm McLaren's fashion boutique, coincidentally called *SEX*. **WOL**

Question 15

Camberwick Green or Trumpton?

CAMBERWICK GREEN: The clown at the beginning added a certain something and the excitement generated by the question of who was going to appear out of the musical box was never matched by the tamer *Trumpton*. *Camberwick Green* starred Mr Windy Miller, the entrepreneur of the Green and a man always ready to fleece his neighbours at the drop of his silly hat. Ask Farmer Bell if you don't believe me. It also had Pippin Fort, housing the trusty men in red; so much more effective than the effete Pugh, Pugh etc., who were too busy singing to put out fires. Camberwick Green housed the better class of puppet and was definitely set in the superior part of Trumptonshire. **CS**

TRUMPTON: I concede that *Camberwick Green* came first, but that's because it was essentially a trial run for the glory that was *Trumpton*. Don't forget - Trumpton was the capital, the NYC, of Trumptonshire, so the exciting stuff happened there and not in the sleepy (and rather too smugly up-market) outposts of Camberwick Green and Chigley. I think it's a great tribute to whoever was Trumpton's fire-prevention officer that there were never any fires for Pugh, Pugh, Barney McGrew, Cuthbert, Dibble and Grubb to put out, so they could entirely dedicate themselves to helping cats out of trees and playing delightful music in the town bandstand. I'd much rather sit in the park with Chippy Minton and enjoy a concert than suffer under the permanent state of martial law that seemed to exist in Camberwick Green. **FM**

Question 16

Big Daddy or
Giant Haystacks?

BIG DADDY: Straight away, can I say that I've always hated wrestling? It is a repugnant waste of everybody's time, so being asked to pick one of these lovelies helped me understand how Hercules felt on a Monday morning.

Big Daddy it is, though. He had what it took to force Giant Haystacks to agree to lose every bout (because let's not kid ourselves, wrestling's more choreographed than *Swan Lake*) over a period of *ten years*. He didn't read the Bible, or have a nasty beard.

His real name was Shirley, which not only makes me laugh like a drain, but also explains why he felt the need to dress in a Lycra baby-gro and intimidate other men.

I must also add that it was due to Big Daddy's misfortune that wrestling disappeared forever from our screens, so for that reason alone he deserves my support. He performed his trademark 'belly splash' manoeuvre on one Mal 'King Kong' Kirk, whose weak heart couldn't take it and the poor man joined the great wrestling fraternity in the sky. But Mal didn't die in vain; Big Daddy retired and the TV companies cancelled their coverage. Every cloud. **CS**

GIANT HAYSTACKS: He was the toughest, he was the roughest, he crushed his opponents with the 'super splash' and they ran screaming as he bellowed, "Don't bring me midgets to wrestle!" at their retreating backs. Bless him, he was always the villain to Big Daddy's so-called good-guy, but the truth was that Haystacks was a real gentleman giant. If he never beat Big Daddy, it was because he wasn't allowed to, thanks to the contrived staging and, oh yes, the fact that Big Daddy's brother was the head booker.

The choice here is between a lovely, big, hairy bloke and a cue-ball in a leotard. I like my wrestlers huge and hirsute, not bald and sweaty, so I'm going with Haystacks. Especially because his cameo appearance in *Give My Regards To Broad Street* is still the greatest performance by a six-foot eleven-inch professional wrestler, in a 1984 British film with music, in the history of cinema. **FM**

Question 17

Basil Brush or Sooty?

BASIL BRUSH: Have you noticed that it wasn't until Basil Brush appeared on our screens that the anti-foxhunting movement really took off? Everybody loved this cheeky, loud-mouthed fox who, by sheer force of personality, proved that his species has so much more to offer than the enthusiastic extermination of chickens. In his little Sherlock Holmes-type coat, he may have looked like an English landed-gentleman, but he was in fact the voice of pure anarchy - which must put him in a winning position over Sooty, who never said anything at all.

Boom! Boom! Ah, how that raucous laugh lit up my Saturday teatimes. Could anyone blunt Basil's rapier tongue? Certainly not the parade of hapless, jobbing actors who had to grin and bear his irreverent teasing. Mr Derek or Mr Roy? Who would you choose? **FM**

SOOTY: While Basil was obviously an aristocrat born into a world of privilege, Sooty was a poor orphan who struggled to break into the cutthroat world of television puppets.

Probably abandoned by his parents for being yellow (not a good colour for a bear), the trauma left him with the inability to master the art of speech. Luckily, the eminent zoologists, Harry and Matthew Corbett, adopted the little scamp and patiently translated his semaphore into English. And if you agree that people can be measured by the quality of their friends, then Sooty definitely makes the grade. First there was Sweep, the Coco Pops magnate, who purposely did no more than squeak in order to make Sooty feel better. And then there was Soo, the sexiest panda glove puppet ever to grace our screens. Watching Sooty helped me to realise how important it is to have good friends around you – especially if you haven't got what it takes to get to the top by yourself. **WOL**

Question 18

Doctor Who:
Pertwee or Baker?

JON PERTWEE: The third and best Doctor. He may have dressed like a Victorian 'friend of Oscar' - and thereby qualifies as the spiritual father of both Vic Reeves and Jonathan Ross - but he had the deportment and manner of a Time Lord. No other Doctor ever managed to represent the quintessence of Time Lordliness quite so convincingly and emphatically. Poor Tom Baker had no other choice than to do something entirely different and whilst I have a great deal of time for Tom, his Doctor unfortunately changed the nature of this programme from terror-inducing to playfully whimsical. I always felt they chose the wrong Baker - the newsreader Richard would have been my choice. **WOL**

TOM BAKER: Tom Baker was, without a shadow of a doubt, the best Doctor of the lot. Everything about him, from the manic eye-rolling to the jelly baby fetish, showed that Tom's Doctor was clearly madder than an entire room full of hatters and far madder than most of his adversaries. But he also exuded immense intelligence and thank God, because it can't have been easy saving Earth every week, with only a slip of girl and a metal dog to help.

Jon Pertwee was lovely, even if he did wear frilly shirts and have hair like an old woman, but he wasn't as convincing, because compared to Tom, he was just too normal. I could really believe that Tom spent his time trolling the darker recesses of the universe, battling with the intergalactic riff-raff. He was also by far the longest-serving Time Lord, and the fact that all the post-Tom Doctors were pale imitations of him proves he was an almost impossible act to follow. **CS**

Question 19

Bagpuss or The Clangers?

BAGPUSS: Just hearing Oliver Postgate's voice makes me want to blub. It conjures up my childhood like almost nothing else, so it must be said that I love both these shows. However, *Bagpuss* wins because of the introduction, particularly when we learn that even though Emily's cat is old, baggy and loose around the seams, she still loves him. Surely there's not a dry eye in the house? I know *The Clangers* was possibly more inventive and made some excellent points about our abuse of the environment, but it doesn't grip my heart and squeeze it till it hurts in quite the same way. **CS**

THE CLANGERS: Sorry, but even though I do a mean impression of the mice in *Bagpuss*, the whole thing left me cold. It was a cat, for a start, and it always looked really grubby. In fact, the whole shop was full of filthy, Victorian junk. It made me feel queasy.
The Clangers, on the other hand, were very clean life forms (not to mention adorable) and their airship was powered by music – how glorious is that? Their whole little world was completely magical and entrancing and I loved it all. I wanted to eat blue string pudding and sup with the Soup Dragon. If aliens ever land on Earth, I hope they're Clangers. The only problem is, they swear like troopers. **FM**

Question 20

The Omen or
The Exorcist?

THE OMEN: Many couples have moments where they wonder if they have given birth to a devil-child, but how can you tell if you actually have? This film helpfully gives some idea of what it would be like.

The Omen indicates that you should begin to suspect trouble shortly after all the people who warn you start dying in various colourful and mysterious ways; your wife is thrown from a hospital window; and you discover your son's real mum was a jackal. What's a father to do?

I also thought it was particularly clever of Satan to choose an American family in which to insinuate his spawn – I mean, how on earth do you start narrowing down precisely which American child it is?

Anyway, *The Omen* wins because *The Exorcist* simply isn't scary. A child goes through a hellish transformation; from a sweet, playful girl to a spitting, swearing, difficult and confrontational daughter of Beelzebub. She turns a funny colour, speaks unintelligibly and upsets the local priests by stabbing at her genitals with a crucifix. Well, I have a sister and none of that seemed particularly unusual to me. **WOL**

THE EXORCIST: Much, much scarier, and isn't that the point? *The Exorcist* is the mother and father of all horror flicks and don't let anyone tell you any different. We have priests doing battle with Satan for the soul of a child; we have a director who fired live rounds on set; and we have a film that was banned for ten years.

By comparison, *The Omen* is horror-lite; it lacks power, guts and any point. *The Exorcist* is arguably one of the most influential films of the twentieth century. *The Omen* does its best, but it's simply out of its league. **CS**

Question 21

Retro Bonds:
Connery or Moore?

SEAN CONNERY: Connery just has 'It' – the quality that makes most men want to be him and most women (and some men) want to be with him.

He doesn't exude good breeding and suave gentility in the way Moore does, but Connery's screen presence is more complex. Beneath the sleek veneer of urbane sophistication lies something dark and brooding, but also supremely capable and self-confident. If I were an agent in trouble, I'd pray for Connery to help me out. If I wanted high tea, cucumber sandwiches and a game of badminton, I'd give Moore a call.

The bad guys don't stand a chance with Connery, because he's Connery, and the ladies don't stand a chance for the same reason. And what about all those terrible chat up lines – who else could get away with those? Yet because he's delivering them, the girls – and sometimes even the boys – just melt. **WOL**

ROGER MOORE: Roger has a sense of humour and a lightness of touch that the dour Scot does not. Then there's the whole body hair issue, which needs to be addressed. Sean looks as though he's stapled several standard poodles to his chest and miniature poodles onto the backs of his hands and his ears. Good God, it's everywhere and it's not pleasant. And if this wasn't enough to instantly convert you to the Moore camp, Sean seems to have mislaid his lips and I can't understand a single word he says. **CS**

Question 22

Space Dust or Flying Saucers?

SPACE DUST: The most exciting sweet ever, and completely unprecedented. Even though it wasn't true that a mouthful of Space Dust taken with a mouthful of Coke would blow your head off (well, you had to try, didn't you?), those millions of minute explosions were definitely the greatest non-chocolate confectionery thrill of the twentieth century.

I can remember the first packet I ever had - orange flavour. It was awesome. Funny to think that fundamentally, the whole miraculous experience was no more than many tiny releases of carbon dioxide. Each mouthful probably blasted a hole in the ozone layer the size of Wales, but somehow, it was worth it.

Flying Saucers have been around forever. They're traditional, not trailblazers. The sherbet is the white stuff you find in Sherbet Fountains and the saucer tastes like it's made out of those shiny, old-style, polystyrene egg-cartons. Flying Saucers are a safe bet, but Space Dust momentarily turned the sweet world upside down. It blew my taste buds, but first it blew my mind. **FM**

FLYING SAUCERS: These were an ingenious way of giving children their recommended daily amount of sherbet in such a way that they wouldn't gag violently as the sweet, lemony powder hit the back of their tiny throats. The strangely textured, saucer-shaped surround was actually a kind of sugary rice-paper which dissolved in your mouth, moistening and containing the powder until the very last second, then voila! A controlled, incident-free sherbet hit.

Space Dust was just a way of increasing the amount of pollutants kids ingested at playtime, in order to make their brains mushy and therefore more susceptible to the propaganda they were force-fed by their teachers. **WOL**

Question 23

Duran Duran or
Spandau Ballet?

DURAN DURAN: They were a proper pop group. They had a lead singer who was sexy, married a model and called his children things like Saffron – everything a front man in a successful band is supposed to do. They even managed to carry off the notoriously precarious New Romantic look. They sang about far off places and made exotic, extravagant videos. Spandau Ballet were pedestrian by comparison; they always looked like they should have been singing in the local pub. They just didn't have the style or flamboyance of Duran Duran. **CS**

SPANDAU BALLET: *Gold* and *True* were generation-defining songs, even if Tony Hadley did leave a slick behind him wherever he went. Spandau Ballet were neither as preening, nor as pretentious as the so-called 'wild boys' (wild boys? Wearing that much make-up?) and thankfully, they all managed to have surnames other than Taylor. If none of this is enough to bring you on side, please also bear in mind that Duran Duran were Diana Spencer's favourite group. Oh, and nobody in Spandau Ballet ever married Amanda de Cadenet. **FM**

Question 24

Ovett or Coe?

STEVE OVETT: Oh, so much better; far more intense and brooding. He combined serious inner demons with great talent. You only had to look at his face - like Munch's *Scream* - to realise he was running for more than mere medals, or a place in the Tory Party. You knew that nothing had ever been easy for Ovett and that made him fascinating. This was no floppy-haired mummy's boy; this was the first (and probably the last) athlete to make running around in circles interesting. Very Tom Courtney; very Alan Sillitoe; very, very good. **CS**

SEB COE: Did you see *Chariots of Fire*? 1924; the Paris Olympics. Two very different British lads are running for their country; they both win a race each; everybody's happy.

Now fast-forward to 1980; the Moscow Olympics. Two very different British lads are running for their country; they both win a race each, but - oh dear! What's all this, now? I never quite understood the origins, or the depth, of the rivalry between these two obviously talented runners, but my guess is that it was all Ovett's fault because he was such a miserable looking bugger. **WOL**

Question 25

Penguin or Club?

PENGUIN: In order to get the full benefit of its magnificence, you must eat it in the correct way. First, slowly lick off the outer layer of chocolate and then do the same to the cream which sandwiches the two, exquisitely crunchy, rectangles together. These you eat last, because they are the *pièce de résistance*. You cannot do this with a Club, mainly because it tastes like a hyena's innards, but also because it falls apart before you can say "Yuck! What foul manner of victual is this?" and throw it in the bin. **CS**

CLUB: If you like a lot of chocolate on your biscuit, welcome! Yes, the chocolate did peel away from the sides a bit, but that's because it was so thick and yummy. And it was fun to have a choice between eating it all at once and dismembering it. What's a Penguin, really? It's just a bourbon, covered in a thin layer of chocolate, but the Club of my childhood was a truly unique combination of biscuit, filling and thick, thick chocolate. And so many different and exciting flavours to choose from! The Club orange was especially sublime. It seems to me that Penguin fans must be very pedestrian, humdrum people, whereas Club devotees are fun-loving adventurers, demanding more from life and picking apart its myriad flavours with a charming gusto. **FM**

Question 26

Swap Shop or Tiswas?

SWAP SHOP: I hated *Tiswas* with a loathing. I may have been no taller than one of Sally James's boots, but even I could see that nobody on *Tiswas* gave a flying flan about me, or anybody else under the age of consent. It was purely for adults and they were selfishly impinging on my sacred Saturday mornings. Whenever I accidentally tuned in, all I ever saw were bored-looking kids, standing around listlessly in the background, while Chris Tarrant and his cackling cronies had the time of their lives. So I switched straight back to *Multi-coloured* (don't ever forget the multi-colours) *Swap Shop*, where I was wanted, where the presenters cared and where I could re-vamp my entire toy cupboard for the price of a phone call. The cartoons were better, too. **FM**

TISWAS: Sally James in denim and thigh-length boots, or Noel Edmonds in his dumb, multi-coloured jumpers? You're joking, right? Apart from Sally's obvious charms, *Tiswas* was also loud and anarchic, involved custard tarts, fart jokes, Spit the dog and the Phantom Flan Flinger. This was kids' TV for real kids, whereas *Swap Shop* was for nerds and cissies. Watching *Tiswas* also ensured you got a few hours bonding time with your dad, who liked to be in the room when it was on (everybody knew why, but nobody said). **WOL**

Question 27

Pretty In Pink or
The Breakfast Club?

PRETTY IN PINK: James Spader - be still, my beating heart - looking scrumptious and Jon Cryer being brilliant. There are no fanciable men in *The Breakfast Club*. Sorry. **FM**

THE BREAKFAST CLUB: I have a soft spot for *Pretty in Pink*, but it doesn't come close to the devotion I feel for the edgier, feistier *Breakfast Club*. Locking all the characters in detention for a few hours was a far more interesting way to tell a story about disaffected, rebellious youth than the usual, boring, girl-meets-boy shtick. The men were so much better too; Judd Nelson wasn't as slimy as James Spader, or as ineffectual as Andrew McCarthy. He was funny, angry and hurting, which of course made him completely irresistible to me. *The Breakfast Club* had Ally Sheedy shaking dandruff out of her hair, a great anthemic song and, for once, Molly's lips were kept firmly in check. **CS**

Question 28

Borg or McEnroe?

BJORN BORG: As a kid, tennis bored me. I neither knew nor cared what went on in that rarefied world. But I knew about Borg.

Borg had a precocious talent (his record of five Wimblebore - sorry, Wimbledon - men's singles titles in a row still stands), but he was also very much his own man. In 1982 he got into trouble with the Men's Tennis Council because he didn't play the required number of tournaments. Borg didn't care; he played tennis because he liked it, not because he had to. So, rather than play to their rules, he retired.

Completely self-confident and cool, Borg was like the older brother I always wished I had. McEnroe was a petulant, stroppy, spoiled brat, just like the little brother I did have.

Anyway, it was never possible to take McEnroe seriously, with his Kelly Le Brock hairstyle and see-my-nuts shorts. Borg wins. **WOL**

JOHN McENROE: The man had a personality; he had fire and brimstone. He made tennis interesting; he was the angry young man of the court; the wild man of Wimbledon. He was far more rock 'n' roll than the boring Borg. His tennis matched his personality - unpredictable and wildly exciting. His weird serve, his bad behaviour and his incredible hair all indicated he was a troubled individual and, where I'm concerned, that's like waving spinach at Popeye. He was driven by inner demons so powerful he couldn't control them, but I was willing to help him. He had the sort of forceful intelligence that's not usually associated with whacking a ball over a net and baby, I'm totally serious. **CS**

Question 29

The Liver Birds or
The Likely Lads?

THE LIVER BIRDS: Sandra, Beryl and Carol provided the backdrop to my childhood. I wasn't aware that this programme was a huge step forward for feminism; I only knew that when I grew up, I wanted to share a flat with my best friend. *The Liver Birds* always seemed bright and optimistic, unlike *The Likely Lads* (or, more specifically, *Whatever Happened to the Likely Lads*), where everybody spent the whole time bemoaning their lot and drinking beer.

The theme songs told you all you needed to know: Terry and Bob's melancholic tune dealt in lost dreams and dashed hopes, while the girls were chirpy, sassy and ever-confident that things would work out for the best. They wore some fantastic outfits, went to parties and generally led what appeared to me (in those days) to be a kick-ass life. Why would anyone prefer to watch two geezers being miserable in Newcastle? **CS**

THE LIKELY LADS: I think you've missed the point about Bob and Terry's strained friendship, which was essentially a metaphor for the development of the British working classes. Whilst one half (Bob) aspired to better themselves by making the transition to besuited middle-management and the trappings of a middle-class lifestyle, the other half (Terry) were left behind, unable or unwilling to change.

Naturally, this appears to be a recipe for disaster, as the inherent strength of the proletariat is essentially divided, diminished and seemingly defeated. But *The Likely Lads* also presented us with a ray of hope for the future, as the common background and experiences shared by Bob and Terry provided a bond that enabled them to overcome, or at least face, their problems together. Apart from the socio-political function of *Whatever Happened to the Likely Lads*, it also had a cracking theme tune.

As for *The Liver Birds*, I can only observe that whilst The Beatles made people think that being Liverpudlian was cool; mopey Sandra, twittering Beryl and the pube-headed Carol all reminded us that it wasn't. **WOL**

Question 30

Flake or Ripple?

FLAKE: This is an outpost of the great "Cadbury or Galaxy?" Question and I'm firmly on side with Cadbury. Flake is sublime; all that dense, cocoa-y chocolate, so delicately packaged and with the treat of a wrapper full of shreds still to come, even after you've finished the main bar. They didn't used to make outrageous commercials about Flake for nothing, you know. It's girl-chocolate *par excellence*. Anyway, Ripple tastes of meat. **FM**

RIPPLE: In general, both these slim, elegant, air-filled chocolate bars are 'treat' chocolate, rather than full-bodied, 'need' chocolate. Bigger, non-aerated bars are what you wolf down at midnight when you're working late, or for elevenses when you're taking a break from building the conservatory. Of these two quintessentially film-watching chocolates, Ripple is my favourite because it's perfectly contained and I can unwrap and consume it without having to watch what I'm doing. I know I won't end up performing lip-gymnastics, trying to stop chocolate shards from falling everywhere and having to lick-pick little bits off my jumper for half an hour after I've finished. The Flake adverts, and the women in them, were great, but they all proved that the Flake is a bar to eat outdoors, or in the bath. Eat one while you're watching the telly and when you get up, it'll look like you left a little skid-mark on the sofa. **WOL**

Question 31

Oasis or Blur?

OASIS: The biggest Question of 1995. I know Oasis often behaved like chimps at a tea party, but Northern pride comes into this. I can't stick up for a load of Southern, art-school nancy boys when there's a half-decent Northern group, trying – failing, but at least trying – to bring back the sounds of the Sixties.

Oasis made things really quite exciting for a moment back there, so I can forgive them a lot for that. What's more, they didn't prat about on stage; they just stood there and played, which was great. None of that cringe-making, sub-Jagger prancing about. Oh, and they never released a record that sounded like Chas 'n' Dave.

But my money is on Oasis mainly because you know that in a fight, they'd have totally gubbed Blur. Oasis's sisters could have gubbed Blur. The Gallagher's mum, single-handed, could have gubbed Blur. And Lord knows, you have to be tough to marry Meg Mathews. **FM**

BLUR: Pity the poor Cockneys. They have but two alternatives: to struggle hard in the battle to be taken seriously, or to give in and make the most of the cheeky-chappie stereotype under which they are forced to labour. Yet miraculously, Blur managed to do both.

Yes, their Cockneyfied tracks (*Country House* and *Parklife*) are irredeemably irritating, but they also managed to produce poignant 'slowies' like *The Universal* and *To the End* and even the barnstorming anthem that is *Song 2*. While Oasis are all about theft (more Beatles anyone?), Blur are all about breadth. Their wider ambitions meant they were bound to get it wrong occasionally, but they avoided being boringly repetitive like their Northern foe.

OK, so they were arty-farty types, but I'd rather that than the endless hard-boy posturing of Liam 'You ****ing ****, I'll smash yer ****ing face in you ****ing ****' Gallagher. **WOL**

Question 32

Barbie or Sindy?

BARBIE: Why am I doing a question on dolls? Well, because I did have dolls as a kid; they were my older sister's cast-offs and they became wives for my Action Man. The first one was about twice the size of Tommy (my Action Man) and had the same hairstyle as Linda Thorson - the Canadian Avenger. This was acceptable only because the doll was passed on to me without any clothes, so Tommy was very happy. But all along, he had his eye on Barbie and why wouldn't he? She was blonde, leggy and nicely, er, balanced.

By the time my sister was ready to give up her Barbie, I was bored of Action Man, but I ensured he got a nice retirement by placing naked Barbie on top of him in a shoebox in the attic. I couldn't tell you the difference between Sindy and Barbie, but I know which one my Action Man fancied and that's good enough for me. **WOL**

SINDY: I was an Action Girl devotee myself, but I did have a Sindy. Don't talk to me about Barbie. I never liked the look of her and that was before I realised she was the ultimate symbol of crass Western vacuousness and an outrageous affront to universal womanhood.

Sindy was a good, British girl. A little chunkier than her transatlantic cousin perhaps, but that was all to the good. Sometimes, she even had brown hair (shock, horror!), but even that well-known doll disability didn't stop her having great clothes and the best horse (even better than Action Girl's).

As far as men are concerned, we all get what we deserve. Barbie is rightly and eternally stuck between super-vacant Ken and inane Blaine; but from 1965-67, Sindy had Paul McCartney for a boyfriend. Plus, she drove an MG. Wow. Lucky Sindy. **FM**

Question 33

Ritz or Tuc?

RITZ: Small discs of heaven. They were the ones my parents served with pâté in the Seventies. They were the ones that came in that fantastic red box. The box that actually made them taste better.

Tuc biscuits were the ones that were too big. They were the ones that were too salty. They were the ones that came in a horrible yellow packet. **CS**

TUC: The class struggle in biscuit form. Tuc (Trades Union Congress) is the worker's choice of biscuit; Ritz is for the pretentious, fancy-pants bourgeoisie.

These are both meant to be biscuits for putting cheese on. Ritz forces you to go looking for small, round, specialist cheeses (thereby depriving you of valuable time for workplace agitation and protest). Tuc, on the other hand, is specifically designed to accommodate your easy-to-find, oblong cheeses – Cheddar, Cheshire, Double Gloucester, Stilton – the favourites of every manual labourer.

The Tuc biscuit also has the advantage of having health and safety corners - the sharp edges being cut off to reduce lunchtime injuries.

Health and safety isn't just a work issue, it's a *workplace* issue. Tuc biscuits represent this eternal truth, so don't let those slave-labour-dependent capitalists fob you off with anything else. **WOL**

Question 34

Scaring yourself:
Toilet Ghost or
Something Under the Bed?

TOILET GHOST: You knew. You knew, from the moment you plucked up the courage to get out of bed, that the Toilet Ghost was waiting. Waiting. Quietly. To get you.

After you'd finished on the loo, you took a deep breath, braced yourself… and flushed. Then you ran, ran like the wind, ran like the hordes of hell were after you – because they were. Everybody knows that the Toilet Ghost will get you if you don't hurl yourself back into bed and hide completely under the covers before the flush finishes.

You can always check and double check that there's nothing under the bed, but even if you're sleeping on the floor, the Toilet Ghost can still get you. That's because the Toilet Ghost can get you wherever you are. There's nowhere to hide from the Toilet Ghost. You know it. Wherever there's plumbing, be prepared to be petrified. **FM**

SOMETHING UNDER THE BED: The Toilet Ghost was scary, but once you realised you could always make it back to bed before the cistern filled up, you knew you'd be OK. Except, that is, for the Something Under the Bed, which was always there, ready to grab your trailing leg – either as you stepped out of bed to go to the toilet, or on the way back. **WOL**

Question 35

Charlie and…
The Chocolate Factory or
The Great Glass Elevator?

THE CHOCOLATE FACTORY: There's the chocolate, of course. Oh, and the chocolate. Any book with so much chocolate has to be a winner. Is there anybody who read this book and didn't go out and buy loads of bars of chocolate, just so they could unwrap them really carefully and pretend there was a golden ticket inside? Single-handedly, Roald Dahl condemned my entire generation to grossly hardened arteries.

It's such a classic, even the Gene Wilder film couldn't ruin it completely. My mouth watered the whole time I was reading it and I still dream that, one day, I'll eat a three-course meal in a piece of gum. I hope to God someone's working on that. How long will it take? How long?

I'd like to mention the *Great Glass Elevator*, but I honestly can't remember a thing about it. **FM**

THE GREAT GLASS ELEVATOR: It's true. There isn't as much chocolate in this superb sequel, but it does have Vermicious Knids. The image of those deadly beasts spelling out the word "scram" has stuck with me to this day. *Great Glass Elevator* also has an American president with a nanny, and a gum fetish, and there's an exciting space capsule rescue. I think that these things more than make up for the fact that there's far less of the sweet stuff and if you can't remember anything about it, then you've not read it. **CS**

Question 36

Palmer or Bond?

HARRY PALMER: He's got to be the choice for those of us who prefer our spies to be fallible, to bleed when they are pricked and to pay for their transgressions. Palmer is a real human being, he doesn't have the Teflon-tough, invincible blandness of Bond. He is captured, he is tortured and there is a real question mark over his survival. Bond is all about chest hair, cocktails and naff gadgets. Palmer made horn-rimmed specs iconic, cooked for his conquests and was miles more interesting. **CS**

JAMES BOND: Harry Palmer was tortured by Albanians. *Albanians.* At least Bond never gets caught by anybody less terrifying than evil, empire-building megalomaniacs with Weapons of Mass Destruction and their own, personal monorails. If it's not happening inside an extinct volcano, it's not happening to Bond. He's cooler, more exciting and the gadgets are great. Harry always looks uncomfortable with his gun – get over it Harry, you're a bleedin' spy for God's sake. I don't want to sit in Harry's seedy little bedsit, watching him chop garlic, when I could be whizzing around Monte Carlo in an Aston Martin with James. OK, I might end up painted gold, but it's a chance worth taking for all the fun I'd have. And if any Albanians attacked, James could see them off with no more than a raised eyebrow. **FM**

Question 37

VHS or Betamax?

VHS: The VHS format was the Microsoft of video. I'm told that the picture quality was never as good, that the machines weren't as sophisticated and that, altogether, it shouldn't have won out against the superior Betamax, but you know what? It did.

I like a winner. Betamax came first, but still lost, so what does that tell you about VHS? Overall, the format was cheaper, the machines were sleeker and the tapes were long enough to - hallelujah! - tape a whole film. It was more user-friendly, as well as being aesthetically pleasing. No one ever failed by keeping things simple.

The success of VHS was proof positive that you don't have to be perfect, so long as you're convenient. It's the mantra of the modern age and Bill Gates was obviously listening. **FM**

BETAMAX: For many people, this debate is the key reference point for an illustration of how the capitalist market system fails the consumer; how the better product can be edged out by the better-marketed product; and how the man-in-the-street is thus cheated out of top-notch technology, only to be cornered into buying stuff that's not so good, but cheaper to produce.

I was too young at the time to be able to verify this and anyway, it isn't even the main point. My main objection to JVC and their VHS system is this: because it won and forced the Betamax system into rapid extinction, all three of my uncles had to fork out for new video recorders within months of buying Betamax. This, they said, had cost them so dearly, they wouldn't be able to afford to buy me any birthday or Christmas presents for the next few years. That's a total of 12 presents I lost out on. Thanks a lot, JVC. **WOL**

Question 38

Yogi Bear or
The Hair Bear Bunch?

YOGI: Yogi Bear became even more celebrated than the US baseball star he was named after. Then he got a bit of Mars named after him. Quite simply, bears don't come much more iconic than this.

Yogi and Boo-Boo might be Fred Flintstone and Barney Rubble in bear form, but their positive contribution to bear-human relations is incalculable. Single-pawed, this one, garrulous, tie-wearing bear compensates Americans for all the occasions when Alaskan grizzlies picnic on their relatives. Indeed, Yogi has long been both an exemplary role model and ambassador for bears everywhere, proving beyond all doubt that what they do in the woods can often be both entertaining and clean.

Last, but certainly not least, Yogi is famous for being smarter than the average bear and let's face it, the Hair Bear Bunch are very, very average bears. **FM**

THE HAIR BEAR BUNCH: They were the coolest, hippest bears in town. They had cool clothes, a cool cave and an invisible motorbike. Their constant breaks for freedom were the sort of maverick, anti-heroic activities that appealed to me, even at an early age. Stealing picnic baskets was very small beer when you compare it to the exploits Hair and the gang got up to, and hell, they were so laid-back, they wouldn't even dream of biting you. **CS**

Question 39

Lolly Gobble Choc Bomb or Fab?

LOLLY GOBBLE CHOC BOMB: Two sweets for the price of one! How can I describe the excitement this caused in my world? Chocolate! On an ice lolly! *In* an ice lolly! It was like Christmas, birthday and the summer holidays rolled into one. Now that Feasts and Magnums are part of everyday life, it's difficult to explain what it meant to have chocolate (with added sugary bits, no less) not only on the outside of some strawberry ice cream, but also to bite into this exotic creation and find – oh my God – an actual chocolate bar in the centre! I've never really recovered. It wasn't even real chocolate, more like baking chocolate, but who cared? It was heaven on a stick.

Fabs were OK and are still very popular among non-connoisseurs, but the Lolly Gobble Choc Bomb – the Adam of the Great Chocolate Lollies - well, it blew the world of ice cream wide open. Things would never be the same again. **FM**

FAB: If it was good enough for Lady Penelope, then it was good enough for me. It involved two (*two*) different flavours of lolly *and* a chocolate coating, liberally dusted with hundreds and thousands. This heady cocktail satisfied all my gastronomic needs at the time. I would have lived off them exclusively, but I failed to convince my parents of their nutritional benefits (shows you what they knew). Watching *Bagpuss* while eating a Fab made me realise that Belinda Carlisle was right - heaven can indeed be a place on earth.

All the Lolly Gobble Choc Bomb had going for it was a ridiculously long name. **CS**

Question 40

Donny Osmond or
David Cassidy?

DONNY: I didn't experience the Osmonds first-hand, but I can appreciate them from a distance and it seems to me that Donny was the ultimate teen-idol. There wasn't a darn thing wrong with him. He was a gent. He obviously flossed. He was even religious. What mother doesn't dream of such a son-in-law?

The problem with David was the sneaking suspicion that maybe he wasn't just non-threatening to girls; maybe he actually *was* a girl. We could be sure Donny wasn't a girl, because we had Marie to compare him with. And to add even more lustre to his legend, whereas Marie was a little bit country, Donny was a definitely a little bit rock 'n' roll. **FM**

DAVID: Unless they had luxurious facial hair, most young men looked liked girls in the Seventies, it was just the way of the world. I'm sure neither of these two would have beaten Anne of Green Gables in an arm wrestling contest, but at least David wasn't so relentlessly wholesome. His teeth didn't look as if they might take over the world, he was in a hit television series, sang better songs and didn't have such a terrible name. **CS**

Question 41

The Jam or The Police?

THE JAM: Along with Buckler on drums and Foxton (the Zaphod Beeblebrox look-alike) on bass, the stripling Weller proved to have a useful talent for kitchen-sink lyrics, in the same London tradition as the Kinks and Squeeze – *That's Entertainment* being the best, but not the only, example.

With such talent, The Jam managed to become the voice, albeit only occasionally and temporarily, of a disaffected and disillusioned generation. OK, so the Police were no mean songsmiths either, and had the charismatic Mr. Sting leading them to global success, but they became self-consciously blond and seemed to think that being pretty would suffice. They proved their contempt for the listening public by releasing *De-Do-Do-Do, De-Da-Da-Da* in 1981. This was so bad, it made the Jam split up (two years later). But while they lasted, The Jam were far edgier, angrier and cooler than the trio of peroxide popsters. **WOL**

THE POLICE: The Question of 1979. Single-for-single, I thought I preferred the Jam, so I went and bought the Greatest Hits of both bands and realised that the Police had a much higher strike-rate. While playing the Jam, I found myself flicking.

The Police were much easier on the eye, too. Andy Summers' nose is exquisite. And while I'm never going to advocate anybody going blond, I can see why they thought it might get them some attention. Not that you need that when your drummer's dad is a CIA bureau chief. (Cool, or what?)

Despite all this, my favourite thing about the Police is the way they sat back and never contradicted the morons who play *Every Breath You Take* at their weddings. It's not their fault people are thick, but watching the world's creepiest stalking song become fashionable as a paean to romantic love must have been quite a laugh. **FM**

Question 42

Thunderbirds or Captain Scarlet?

THUNDERBIRDS: The Tracy family owned an island, the lads were named after early American astronauts and they got to drive the most fantastic vehicles. It still makes the hairs on the back of my neck stand on end when I hear that music and watch Thunderbird One emerge from the bowels of the swimming pool. You knew then that the day was well on the way to being saved and The Hood's evil plans had only moments to live.

I found the perfect female role model in Lady Penelope. She had the biggest, pinkest car in the world and still managed to be a successful international spy. If that's not having your fairy cake and eating it, I'd like to know what is. She had the sort of style and class that the slutty *Captain Scarlet* girls could only dream of. You don't call yourselves ridiculous names like Harmony and Rhapsody unless you want it to be universally known that you're always free in the evenings and charge by the hour. And how many puppet shows can claim to be the inspiration for a real life, international rescue team, as *Thunderbirds* was? Not many, that's for sure, and certainly not *Captain Scarlet*. **CS**

CAPTAIN SCARLET: He's indestructible. **FM**

Question 43

Chopper or Grifter?

CHOPPER: This was the bike for me. I fell in love for the first time with a boy who rode a Chopper. It was his brother's, so it had seen better days, but to my young eyes it was the coolest thing ever, and so was he. I blame the bike entirely. It was the Under Ten's equivalent of a Harley Davidson and, as such, commanded great respect. Everybody who rode one instantly became a miniature Dennis Hopper in *Easy Rider* and even though this particular model was a rather dubious shade of bright, bright yellow, it still managed to convey the notion that its owner was mad, bad and dangerous to know. The Grifter might have been the better bike for all sorts of technical reasons, but who cares about that? **CS**

GRIFTER: I'm not convinced by the *Easy Rider* analogy. The Chopper was more like a circus-monkey's bike, with its 'banana' seat and 'ape-hanger' handlebars. Great for riding around in circles and doing wheelies for twenty minutes or so, but damned uncomfortable if you actually wanted to go cycling anywhere other than the street in front of your house.

In evolutionary terms, the Chopper was to bicycles what Sigue Sigue Sputnik were to music – not even a novelty, but a freakish aberration; a dead end from which the only way forward was to go back and try to forget you'd ever been there.

The Grifter was the dawn of a new hope. Both mankind and bicycles had overcome the fundamental error of their ways, universal equilibrium was restored and the descent into madness was avoided - for the time being. And anyway, the Grifter had a twist-grip gearshift - how great is that? **WOL**

Question 44

The Avengers or
The New Avengers?

THE AVENGERS: I wouldn't say no to Joanna Lumley, but *The Avengers* had an incomparable range of skirt to choose from – a delectable trio of leather-clad, whip-wielding lovelies. You can't ignore that kind of lure. The plots were weirder, the cars were better and there were more girls. That's all I need. I also can't forget that my childhood was scarred by having Gareth Hunt shake his beans at me. I'm still recovering. **WOL**

THE NEW AVENGERS: I don't have any nostalgia for the original series, as I wasn't around when it aired, but I've seen the repeats and frankly, it's incomprehensible. Despite being barely rooted in reality, it still failed to capture my imagination. *The New Avengers* at least had some pizzazz: Purdey's iconic hair-do, car chases, snappy dialogue, proper location shooting and Gareth Hunt, adding a bit of much-needed machismo. Steed was always far too effete for me. But most importantly, this series didn't need to rely on PVC and S&M to maintain our interest. **CS**

Question 45

The Hitchhiker's Guide
to the Galaxy
or Red Dwarf?

THE HITCHHIKER'S GUIDE: Herein lie the answers to all the great philosophical and scientific questions; from the meaning of life, to how the universe began - and ended. I would be lost without it, especially when I'm trying to put together a decent fjord.

The Hitchhiker's Guide is a vital handbook for existence. What does *Red Dwarf* tell anybody, except that heaven must surely be a dreadlocked-Scouser-free zone?

Also, because *The Hitchhiker's Guide* is a book, a television series, a radio play and really easy to mime, it's the perfect choice for a game of charades. **FM**

RED DWARF: *Red Dwarf* was the first space-based sit-com. This gave it lots of scope for being brilliant and inventive, but also for getting things spectacularly wrong. Luckily for everybody, it didn't get much wrong at all. With a great premise - the power struggle between the sole survivor of a radioactive leak, re-awakened after three million light years in space, and his companions (a hologram of his dead, much-loathed room-mate; a highly-evolved humanoid cat; a senile computer and a mechanoid that wants to be human) - the series manages to be edgy and streetwise, as well as outrageous and subversive (like the fact that their current vessel, the Starbug, is made from the same material as those plastic dolls that survive plane crashes).

The Hitchhiker's Guide was great, but it was also very middle-class; *Red Dwarf* is a dark and droll version of *Star Trek*. It works for me. **WOL**

Question 46

Christmas Songs:
Wizzard or Slade?

I WISH IT COULD BE CHRISTMAS EVERY DAY: Wizzard were a strange lot and their singing a Christmas anthem is stranger still. That hair and those glasses told me there was something else going on besides Yuletide cheer, which is why this has to be my choice.

The Slade song has none of the subversive qualities that Roy Wood brought to *I Wish It Could Be Christmas Every Day*. It's too loud and too bouncy to be bearable. When all's said and done, it's just a bunch of sideburns announcing what the shops have been telling us since Bank Holiday Monday. **CS**

MERRY CHRISTMAS EVERYBODY: Surely, *the* Christmas song? When Noddy yells "Iiit's Chriiiiiistmaaaass!" you can be absolutely sure it is. It's always a thrill, hearing the first Noddy-yell of the season. It warms me cockles, it does.

Do we really wish it were Christmas every day? I don't. If it were Christmas every day, we'd all be obese paupers. It's not a nice wish, Roy. In fact, it's downright unpleasant, so stop it. And while I'm here, what's all that stuff at the end about the snowman bringing the snow? If there was no snow before the snowman brought it, how can there be a snowman at all? How can something that relies upon snow for its very existence be the same thing that brings the snow into existence? It's an upsetting, chicken/egg dilemma that has already kept me awake on too many Christmas Eves. Enough is enough. **FM**

Question 47

Hill Street Blues or NYPD Blue?

HILL STREET BLUES: The original and best. *Hill Street* said it first and said it all; nothing else comes close. You can't overestimate its impact. It had more than two main characters, the scripts were strong, witty and sophisticated, it was brilliantly acted and its immortal catch phrase still reminds me to be careful whenever I venture forth.
NYPD Blue is good, but it's just another version of *Hill Street*. The camera shakes more and the characters have different names, but essentially we're watching the same programme. Although without the great theme tune. **CS**

NYPD BLUE: OK, so *Hill Street Blues* was groundbreaking stuff, but I feel it was mainly a testing ground for Steve Bochco. *NYPD Blue* is where the ingénue finally became the master. *Hill Street* was part drama and part comedy (or 'dramedy'), which isn't quite what I'm looking for from my US cop series. *NYPD* was grittier and darker, and although it may have relied too heavily on two main characters (Simone and Sipowitz), there were many more reasons to watch. Other than the great scripts, the wonderful acting and the all-pervading, brooding suspense, there was also the delectable Detective Diane Russell. Never has a damaged, dysfunctional alcoholic seemed such an attractive prospect. She could handcuff and beat me any time. **WOL**

Question 48

Herbie or
Chitty Chitty Bang Bang?

HERBIE: Name me one thing that Chitty Chitty Bang Bang can do that Herbie can't. I've no grudge against anybody's fine, four-fendered friend, but Chitty is a one-film car and what's more, it looks worryingly like some bat-car contraption that Dick Dastardly might drive in *Wacky Races*.

Essentially, Chitty is a glorified get-away vehicle. The story isn't about the car; it's about those lisping brats getting kidnapped. (Three cheers for the Child Catcher!) Herbie, on the other hand, is a bona fide hero. He's the whole point of watching those films. For about a year after I saw *Herbie Rides Again*, all my car journeys were spent counting VW Beetles. (Well, it was better than I Spy.)

Herbie was a person, not a means of transport. He was brave, generous, bright and funny, but he also got mad, jealous, drunk and even. Think about it – Chitty Chitty Bang Bang is an 'it', but Herbie is forever a 'he'. Dogs might pee on hubcaps, but what other car oils on the baddie's leg? Everybody adores Herbie – they don't call him the Love Bug for nothing. **FM**

CHITTY CHITTY BANG BANG: I genuinely cannot understand why anyone could, or would, prefer Herbie. Chitty is the magical car, the beautiful car, the fairytale car, the car that would fly you to far-off, exciting places. Chitty was an old racing car, lovingly rebuilt by an inventor for his children, so it had a romantic and spiritual heritage. Herbie had no such pedigree. It was a crap car, in crap, slapstick films and should have had something heavy dropped on it from a great height. Did anyone write a timeless song about the Volkswagen? No, they did not. **CS**

Question 49

Kerplunk or Buckaroo?

KERPLUNK: Kerplunk is a game of true skill and, in comparison with Buckaroo, it proves a suspicion I've had ever since first-year maths, which is that any idiot can add, but you need real intelligence to take away.

Yet Kerplunk is also a superb metaphor for life and the resilience of the human spirit. With every straw we withdraw, we know our world could come crashing down, yet still, on, on we go; pulling, pulling, despite the profound, inescapable understanding that one day, we will pull the last straw and yea, the hell-marbles will fall upon us from a great height. It's nail-biting stuff; a walk on the wild side; a brush with the eternal.

My Buckaroo broke on Boxing Day. I'd only added the bucket and the rope. I can neither forgive nor forget. **FM**

BUCKAROO: I'm with Father Ted on this one. Buckaroo is indeed the sport of kings. **WOL**

Question 50

Illya Kuryakin or Napoleon Solo?

ILLYA: Small, blond and as cute as a button. From the moment I encountered the UNCLE agents, he was always the one that caught my eye. My first erotic dream involved a frisking by Mr Kuryakin, and a girl doesn't forget these things. He managed to convey that beneath his refrigerator-cool, reserved exterior, lay a volcano, and boy, did I want to be the one to bring along the de-icer. He had a wonderful, if random, Eastern European accent (Russian, supposedly. Who cared?), which added a shot of exoticism into the already heady cocktail. Solo wasn't unappealing in his own way, but he was just too smooth and shared too many facial characteristics with a cod to make this heart skip a beat. **CS**

NAPOLEON: They're both so lovely, sometimes it's difficult to know which way to look, but in the end, I think it boils down to a question of female maturity. When you're very young, Illya is the ultimate Non-Threatening Male. He looks like an angel and you're quite safe with him. You can try to kiss him all you like, but he'll never kiss you back. He's the perfect, remote, untouchable ice-idol. At this stage of your life, you're quite right to mistrust dark, predatory men who look like they'd do unspeakable things to you, given half the chance. Then you get older and suddenly, giving dark, wicked men half a chance becomes a much more interesting option. **FM**

Question 51

Mods or Rockers?

MODS: The pitched battles between Mods and Rockers in the Sixties were, in reality, a final showdown between Homo sapiens and Neanderthals. Mods were the progressive, cultured sapiens, who delighted in the symbols of human progress by wearing sharp suits, riding around on fantastic Italian Lambrettas and Vespas, and listening to intelligent, multi-cultural music. The Rockers wore crudely decorated animal skins, rode around on souped-up Nortons and BSAs - the Sixties equivalent of war-beasts - and were unable to cope with anything other than basic musical arrangements.

The descendents of the Neanderthal Rockers can still be seen occasionally, in some British city centres. They are the black-clad Goths. Now subdued and seemingly harmless, these mumbling miserablists shuffle around at night, looking sad and forlorn. But don't try to stroke them, for they are bitter in defeat; they carry dagger-crucifixes and have grown strong by drinking the blood of dead cats. **WOL**

ROCKERS: The Beatles started out as Rockers, before they went on to become Mockers. This alone is enough to recommend the greasy lads over the prissy Mods, whose nice, clean hair really isn't enough to outweigh the school uniform parkas and girly scooters.

Basically, I'm asking myself, if I were on Brighton beach in 1964 and both lots were knocking the hell out of each other, which would I put money on? The big, leathery biker-blokes with chains and knuckle-dusters, or the mohair-suit brigade, who are so busy comparing cufflinks that they fail to reach their get-away Vespas before some massive, crepe-soles come crashing down on their freshly blow-dried heads? Even if a Mod did get hold of a Rocker, he'd never be able to get a grip because of all the Brylcreem.

Anyway, if it comes down to Elvis or The Who, the King wins. **FM**

Question 52

The Lone Ranger or Zorro?

THE LONE RANGER: I think *The Lone Ranger* wins for three reasons:
1. It made a positive contribution to American socio-cultural relations (as one of the first TV programmes to cast a Native American as a hero, albeit a sidekick).
2. Despite its daytime slot, it had a nicely macabre tinge to it (the Lone Ranger's mask was made from his dead brother's vest).
3. It has provided the best answer I've ever heard to a trivia quiz question. When asked: "Who was the Lone Ranger's sidekick?" My friend, Mary, started rolling her eyes and tapping her head with her forefinger. "Ooh, I know this one, I know this one." Moments passed with no answer, just more tapping and "Ooh, I know it! Ooh, ooh, what's his name?" The minutes ticked away and we were about to say that her time was up, when suddenly she sat bolt upright, with her finger in the air and a look of wild joy on her face. "I know! I know!" she squealed. "Cocky!" **WOL**

ZORRO: From the opening credits, when I saw his sword expertly etch out a "Z", I knew it was going to be good and indeed, I was right. There was a colossal amount of swaggering; lots of bellowing laughter, involving heads being thrown back; a fine moustache; some spectacular sword play; and a good cape. It would have been rude to ask for more. I'm glad I saw the re-runs of *Zorro* when I was young, and was mostly spared *The Lone Ranger*. God, he looked boring; riding around in a boring desert, on a boring horse, with a boring name that didn't mean 'fox' in Spanish. I wanted style, I wanted panache - not some lumpy cowboy with a rubbish mask and a nasty shirt. **CS**

Question 53

Muhammed Ali or George Foreman?

ALI: I can hardly begin to tell you how much I admire this man. Physically supreme, extremely brave and tactically masterful, he turned boxing from a sport where two men shuffle around slugging away at each other, into an exhilarating, genuinely popular form of entertainment.

Ali was just as brave out of the ring as he was in it. He was the first national figure to speak out against the Vietnam war and, while some non-combatants went on to become President, Ali's refusal to be drafted saw him stripped of his boxing title, his passport, his boxing licence and facing five years imprisonment.

I know that lots of people, especially women, found the brashness and bragging of the 'Louisville Lip' too much to take, but this was all part of the performance. So what if he came across as a little egotistical? His talent was so great, the boasts were as true as they were funny. The best illustration of this was after the 'rumble in the jungle', which Ali won, despite the fact that his career was in decline and Foreman's was in the ascendancy. He declared: "When you're as great as I am, it's hard to be humble." **WOL**

FOREMAN: As far as I'm concerned, this is a "Star or Survivor?" Question. Pretty boy Ali can sting like a bee until the cows come home, but even if he does claim to be 'the Greatest', he'll never be 'King of the Grill'.

The fact is that Foreman not only has 76 wins to Ali's 56 (with more knockouts and an equal number of losses), he's also the oldest man ever to be World Heavyweight champion, since he won the title for the second time at the age of forty-six.

I like a survivor, especially one who campaigns against litter. Ali's posing got boring, but Big George is still preaching away and threatening to come back and punch another (younger) man's lights out. And he probably could. But please George, cut out the meat will you? The fat might drain away, but the dodgy hormones are still in there. **FM**

Question 54

Play School or Play Away?

PLAY SCHOOL: *Play School* got me through the week. It was a warm, fuzzy, security blanket that I could curl up in, as I waited with bated breath to go through the arched window (the Jaclyn Smith of the windows - definitely superior to the round or the square, the Farrah or the Kate, but bizarrely, the one least talked about).

I was always ready to play, whatever the day, but *Play Away* was an entertainment too far. I remember being incredibly excited about watching it and then thinking, hang on – this is Saturday. Watching a *Play School* spin-off, however light-hearted, while *Grandstand* was on the other side, just made the weekend into an unsatisfactory extension of the week. Thanks, Brian, but no thanks. Take your jaunty jingles elsewhere. Saturdays were special. Saturdays were for *The Banana Splits*, wrestling and Bette Davis films on BBC2. None of the merry japes that you, Jonathan and Jeremy got up to could ever alter that precious status quo. **FM**

PLAY AWAY: I never really hit it off with *Play School*. I never gave a monkey's what was behind either the door or the window, nor did I care if they were round or square. I never reacted well to earnest programmes that wanted me to learn, which is why I would play away, but not at school. *Play School* is a contradiction in terms; learning isn't playing, even if it involves some toys and a man pretending to blow himself up like a balloon.

Play Away was straightforward and didn't sneak in any attempts to make me use my little grey cells. I was given music, laughter, Jonathan Cohen and a good time. **CS**

Question 55

Transformers:
Autobots or Decepticons?

AUTOBOTS: If you want to know the real and living truth of world history, but can't afford the fees charged by the Church of Scientology, just buy into the story of the Transformers, which (I'm told) is pretty similar. Apparently, the Transformers crash-landed on Earth millions of years ago, only to be recently re-activated. They now continue their battle of good versus evil pretty much in secret, but the Decepticons have begun targeting humans and the friendly Autobots are trying to protect us. It can be reassuring to think that the innocuous delivery van outside your house could well be Ironhide, a friendly Autobot, making sure that the innocent-looking bull ambling down the street isn't really Tantrum, an evil Predacon.

Aware that John Travolta and Tom Cruise could possibly be top Autobots (turning into a motorbike and a sidecar respectively), I began to hope that one day I would discover that my Dad was really Optimus Prime, their brave leader and, occasionally, a truck. It took me a long time to accept that he really was just an ordinary bloke, who sometimes sat on a tractor. Despite that disappointment, I still live in hope that I will one day meet and marry a sexy Fembot, preferably one who turns into a Porsche 911 Turbo S. **WOL**

DECEPTICONS: Even when dealing with robots, it has to be said that baddies are so much more interesting and attractive than good-guys. The Decepticons were the best; from the tops of their evil robot heads, down to the tips of their evil robot toes. They had better names and could transform themselves into far more macho and useful things than an elephant, or a hatchback. Hatchbacks simply aren't scary.

There is even a Decepticon porn site, where you get to see nasty robots doing all sorts of even nastier things to each other. If I am forced to have anything at all to do with Transformers, I'll throw in my lot with the wanton and depraved ones and not with the happy-clappy, do-gooder Autobots. **CS**

Question 56

Vinyl or CD?

VINYL: Vinyl records were the primary music medium of my youth and they were perfectly fine. My first record was *DK50/80* by John Otway and Wild Willy Barrett and I still remember the hairs on the back of my neck tingling with expectancy as the stylus slowly clicked its way around the groove before it hit the first note.

Then, one evening, *Tomorrow's World* revealed that vinyl records were to become a thing of the past. The future was here and it was small and shiny. This alone suggested technological superiority over the simple vinyl record. Judith Hann revealed all: you could drop it, scratch it with a knife, spread jam on it, or use it as a dinner plate. It didn't matter what you did, the CD would still play.

The debate still rages over whether or not CDs are better than vinyl and I have to say, I'm not too sure I would have noticed - without prompting - that CDs capture a narrower range of frequencies than vinyl, producing a much flatter and tinnier sound. I just know that I miss the slow clicking of the stylus in the record groove before it hits the first note. And anyway, I never felt that it was really such a drawback of vinyl that you couldn't spread jam on it. **WOL**

CD: Much easier to store, better sound quality and you don't have to fanny about with turntables, needles and all that bollocks. Those who cling onto vinyl are contrary, difficult folk who refuse to embrace change. They will put everything into alphabetical order, get all twitchy if you start to fiddle with their collection and probably still live with their mother. They should be avoided like a rat with a pustule. **CS**

Question 57

Fingerbobs or Potty Time?

FINGERBOBS: *Fingerbobs* and *Potty Time* were two of the weirdest programmes ever made, but the latter was too manic for me. I preferred the rather more gentle adventures of Fingermouse, Scampi, Gulliver, et al. I was young; it didn't even occur to me to wonder if the man presenting it might be mad as a bag of snakes. I had no idea how very odd those paisley scarves and that beard actually were. He had a lovely voice, wore different coloured gloves and told wonderful stories. I didn't need to know any more. It was the perfect programme to watch while eating my lunch. Even now, if someone mentions *Fingerbobs*, I automatically feel hungry and long for some mince and peas.

Potty Time just made me feel anxious. I don't trust a puppet if I can't see its eyes. **CS**

POTTY TIME: This programme provided a unique, televisual insight into the bizarre imaginings of a mad Peruvian.

Michael Bentine's *Potty Time* was a series of plays - often re-enactments of classic stories such as *The Man in the Iron Mask*, *The Invisible Man* and *The Great Escape* - by a team of Hasidic Jewish puppets (enormous hats and masses of facial hair).

Although strange, this show had the best special effects of any hand-puppet show on television. I will never forget the magical appearance of the Invisible Man's footprints in the sand, or the way little bits of dust were kicked up by the puppets whenever they 'ran' across the set.

I never really understood what was going on, but I suspect that the title of this programme was a hint that you should really only try watching it after a few puffs on some of Peru's finest *Cannabis sativa*. **WOL**

Question 58

Star Trek:
Classic or
Next Generation?

CLASSIC: Never let it be said that I wouldn't defend the NCC 1701-D to the death, but if truth be told, my heart still lies with the first Enterprise.

It's the derring-do, you see. In the *Next Generation* there's lots of do, but not so much derring, and I love a bit of derring, especially when there's added do. I quite understand why it's a bad idea for the captain of a starship to risk his life by leaving the bridge, but this means he never gets to beam down to the surface, beat the crap out of a lump of angry silicon and get his shirt picturesquely torn in the process. You never saw a nipple on the *Next Gen*. Nobody got their vest ripped to shreds. Not even Riker. Believe me, I've checked.

Classic *Star Trek* blazed a great, multicultural trail that *Next Gen* continued, but I love it best because it's in-yer-face fun. Nobody sits around in conference, agonising about the Prime Directive and serving ambassadors cups of Earl Grey. No, they save the universe by beaming down to the planet, losing a crew-member, chucking some polystyrene rocks about and being heart-stoppingly heroic. Oh, and you've got to love that Technicolour. Everything is *so* much brighter. **FM**

NEXT GENERATION: If I could choose which captain to serve under, I'd have no hesitation in requesting cool, calm, intelligent Picard over passionate, emotional, tubby, bewigged Kirk. I would also choose the *Next Generation* because, although the original *Star Trek* was groundbreaking for its core values of inter-racial and inter-species tolerance, *Next Gen* went a step further and - thanks to Riker and Worf - challenged the long-held prejudice that people with beards can't be good guys.

I particularly love *Next Gen* for the moments when some nasty species calls up the bridge of the Enterprise to say "Surrender, human filth, or we will destroy your ship!" and the resident empath, Counsellor Troi, gives her usual, profound insight: "I sense hostility, Captain."

Lastly, *Next Gen* wins for episode twenty-one of the fifth season alone, in which the fantastic Famke Janssen plays Kamala, an empathic metamorph – a rare creature born with the ability to sense what her mate desires and become what he wants her to be. Beam me up now! Right now! **WOL**

Question 59

Pogo stick or
Space Hopper?

POGO STICK: Being short of stature, I didn't have the length of leg to properly get to grips with a Space Hopper, but then again, I never really wanted to. They were so undignified, so orange and so very, very pointless. At least with a pogo stick you could bounce around with some modicum of dignity. Then there was the added kudos of actually being able to use it, unlike so many of my less well-balanced playground companions. It's one of the few things I've ever been really, really good at and I can't put it on my CV. Oh, what the hell, I'll put it under 'hobbies'. **CS**

SPACE HOPPER: The past was bright; the past was orange - with horns and a big-toothed face painted on it, although I hardly noticed the face at the time. Looking at it now, it could well be an ancient Babylonian representation of the Rabbit Devil of Death, but miraculously, I never turned into Donnie Darko.

You couldn't go very fast, or bounce very high, but there was something about the Space Hopper that made it completely indispensable. I think it was the comfort factor. Standing about with your mates, not knowing what to do next, could be a bit boring - but if you were all lolling around on your Space Hoppers, you were already playing. Everybody agreed, it was a good place to put your legs and no back garden of the Seventies was complete without at least one lying around on the grass.

Pogo sticks might be fun, I don't know. I've never managed to stay on one for more than three seconds. **FM**

Question 60

Threesomes: Hector's House or Andy Pandy?

HECTOR'S HOUSE: This is about sexism, pure and simple. In *Hector's House*, the women ruled. Yes, we might all have prayed for silly old Hector to take his shotgun and blast that damned frog off her wall, but the fact remained that Kiki and ZaZa were liberated women who did pretty much whatever they liked. Amiable old Hector just gardened around them as they lounged about, bitching, giggling and drinking like fishes. Contrast this with *Andy Pandy*, in which two feral males carouse without restraint, all the livelong day. Until the blessed moment when Andy and Teddy disappear, Looby Loo is condemned to sit slumped in her chair, inert and folorn. Only when she's alone and freed from such repression can she come to life, dance, sing - oh yes, and clean up after the lazy little sods.
Not only were Hector's girls inspirational, he also won our admiration for his good-natured self-mockery. Big old loveable Hector was a gent, he was. **FM**

ANDY PANDY: I'm not sure that bitching and bossing don't also conform to a sexual stereotype, and one that's far worse than the image of woman as homemaker. Looby Loo might have indulged in a little light dusting, but at least she didn't henpeck her housemates. Instead of haranguing her male companions, she quietly opted out and waited for the moment when Andy and Teddy decided to do something to their cart before she danced and played. She was an independent rag doll and didn't need male approbation – she just did her own thing. Given that Andy was dressed as a deckchair and Teddy was clearly up to no good, who can blame her? You go, girl! **CS**

Question 61

School tie knot: large or tiny?

LARGE: It was a way of celebrating my burgeoning sexuality; it was saying to the world that this girl was well on the way to becoming all woman. So you see, it was important to make the knot as large as possible. It doesn't pay to be subtle when dealing with men.

Those who went with the small knot were clearly stating that they had chosen a life of repression and cat-loving spinsterhood. They were not people you could discuss Simon Le Bon's inside leg measurement with, or ponder the clear advantage Doyle had over Bodie, for the simple reason that they had given up on everything that was important in life. **CS**

TINY: Don't you ever, ever accuse me of liking cats. Luckily for you, we tiny-knotters were above such infantile, playground name-calling. We were the minimalist intellectuals. The tinier your knot, the longer it lasted. If you could keep one perma-knot going all year, and your mum had to pick it undone with tweezers, you were a contender.

Ours was a streamlined look; we thought and moved fast, unlike the louche, fashion-victims who went for large. What sort of moron chooses a tie knot that needs to be done afresh every day? Big-knotters also tended to be disciples of the asymmetrical fringe and cheap earrings. You just knew the girls in the Human League would have had big knots.

As for boys, there was something unpleasantly dandyish and New Romantic about the big-knotters – possibly because they were almost sporting cravats. No schoolboy will ever qualify as articulate, but at least the tiny-knotters could always be relied upon to quote Paul Weller lyrics – thus proving they understood multi-syllabic words. **FM**

Question 62

Airwolf or Knight Rider?

AIRWOLF: *Airwolf* was OK, but I'm choosing it because I hated *Knight Rider*. A man with tight jeans and a perm, prancing around America with an effete car that obviously fancied him, was too much for my impressionable young mind. Am I the only one who noticed that every time Michael met a pretty girl, his car would say: "Hmm, I don't trust her, Michael"? I think the programme makers seriously misunderstood the idea of the perfect union of man and machine, which is supposed to be a metaphor for technological progress and human advancement, not a bizarre, sexual sub-text. For those not convinced that KITT fancied Michael, consider why the producers picked William Daniels to be the voice of KITT. William's previous work had involved appearances in such films as *Captain Nice* and *All Night Long*. Now think about KITT purring: "Quick, get inside me Michael!" and you can't fail to see what *Knight Rider* was really about.

This was a programme for men who could look at a photograph of a woman doing the hoovering in a skimpy little French maid's outfit and then start fantasising about the hoover. Sick. **WOL**

KNIGHT RIDER: The helicopter couldn't talk. It couldn't tell you when to pull off the motorway, it couldn't remind you to pick up a pint of milk and I'm sure it didn't have grappling hooks. It would also be a bugger to park outside Sainsbury's.

Airwolf did have the lovely Jan Michael Vincent, but he wore a horrible boiler suit and a silly helmet, which cancels out any 'cooler leading man' advantage it might otherwise have had. So, no. I can't think of a single reason why anyone would choose the helicopter over the car, unless of course they were trying to wean themselves off car porn. **CS**

Question 63

Zoo Time or Animal Magic?

ZOO TIME: In 1637, the French idiot Rene Descartes tried to create a philosophy that would show humankind to be the "masters and possessors of nature". During the course of his arguments, he contended that animals were stupid because they couldn't make humans understand what they were saying, if indeed they were saying anything at all. Johnny Morris may have been trying to address this terrible error by giving a voice to the thoughts and actions of his zoo animals, but he was tragically misguided; not only because we knew it was his voice all along, but also because his anthropomorphism gave animals and their behaviour a value only in the context of their being human-like. Johnny played right into Descartes' hands.

Although it was an earlier attempt to undo the damage the mad French philosopher had wrought, *Zoo Time* took a far more modern approach, with Dr Desmond Morris attempting to show and explain the innate behavioural instincts of animals. This was a far more enlightened attitude than Johnny Morris's bizarre, off-stage ventriloquism. **WOL**

ANIMAL MAGIC: I loved this when I was little. Of course, the very best bit was Johnny Morris, providing the voices for the animals in Bristol Zoo. I thought this was the funniest thing I'd ever heard. The only sections of the programme I didn't like were the bits where Tony Soper (and latterly the man with the strange hair, Terry Nutkins) tried to actually teach me something about nature. I really couldn't be doing with that at all. I wanted more Dotty the lemur and less lecturing, thank you very much. Had *Zoo Time* still been around when I was a kid, it would have been far too earnest and solemn to have made my 'to watch' list. *Animal Magic* was just what it said it was. **CS**

Question 64

Tufty Club or
Green Cross Code Man?

TUFTY CLUB: The tragic image of Willy Weasel's dropped ice cream cone, slowly melting in the middle of the road after yet another of Willy's close motor-related shaves, will never leave me. God bless Tufty and his selfless little woodland friends for showing me the road-safety light. Thanks to their excellent example, I'm still here, with all my limbs intact. No way will I ever go to the ice cream van without my mum. Not after what happened to Willy.

The Green Cross Code Man may have occasionally needed robots to help him out, but generally, his Lycra-clad bulk was solid and reassuring. Then something dreadful happened. The next time I saw him, he was rasping away inside some sort of black, portable iron-lung, obviously the result of a terrible accident caused by not looking right, left, then right again, when crossing the road. What sort of role model was that? Then there was his standoffish instruction to pay attention "…Because I won't be there when *you* cross the road". No, you never were, Green Cross Code traitor. You left us high and dry. Ah, but Tufty…whenever I reach the kerb, I feel his paw in mine. **FM**

GREEN CROSS CODE MAN: Growing up in the countryside, I would often go out walking or cycling and, on most occasions, I'd chance across a small, furry animal that had been squished into the road by a car, tractor, or combine harvester. Yet in all that time, I never recall coming across a squished, well-built man; and certainly not one wearing spearmint-coloured Spandex. As a result, I have always assumed that when it came to the difficult task of crossing the road, it would be better to take advice from a well-built man, rather than from a rodent. **WOL**

Question 65

Beckenbauer or Cruyff?

BECKENBAUER: It's not easy to pick 'the Kaiser' over Cruyff. People might see this as picking efficiency over beauty, and to a certain extent that is true, but you'd be doing Beckenbauer a disservice to characterise his football as simply a sporting version of *Vorsprung durch Technik*. He was a joy to watch. Maybe he wasn't as awe-inspiring as Cruyff, with his flashes of brilliance, but Beckenbauer was consistent in the display of his talent; elegant on the ball and tactically brilliant.

But football is not only about playing well. It's about winning and this is where he outshines Cruyff. He was captain of Germany when they won the World Cup in 1974 (against Holland and Cruyff) and manager when they won in 1990. The fact that he was the first person ever to win the World Cup both as player and manager is testament to his skill. Oh, and he won in 1990 by beating the Argies. Hooray! **WOL**

CRUYFF: The Total Footballer. The centre forward of centre forwards. The great intuitive, spiritual, footballing genius. Cruyff's skills on the pitch are legendary, but that's not why I choose him. He's the best of the best because he was enough of an individual to tear the centre stripe out of the three stripes on his Adidas-sponsored shirt. I'd like to claim that Cruyff, alone of his entire, greed-ridden profession, had nobly refused to be a marketing tool, but unfortunately, he did it because he already had a personal deal with Puma. **FM**

Question 66

The Addams Family or
The Munsters?

THE ADDAMS FAMILY: Obviously, it's finger-clickin' good, but I vote Addams because when I was young, I was Wednesday. I couldn't help it. Initially, I didn't even know she existed, but I was her and I have the photos to prove it. Once Channel 4 screened repeats, I realised I'd found my destiny. I knew I wasn't a decorative child, but that didn't matter once I saw I had the potential to become another Morticia; queen of creepy chic, mistress of all I surveyed (from the comfort of my black velvet chaise-longue) and finger-clicker extraordinaire. I determined there and then to spend my adulthood lightly decapitating roses and being adored by my besotted husband. I've never regretted it. All the Addams family are to be respected, but Morticia is the woman; the ultimate role model for brunettes everywhere. Unlike the hillbilly *Munsters*, *The Addams Family* is forever a blonde-free zone. **FM**

THE MUNSTERS: OK, there was a blonde in *The Munsters*, but it was the fantastic Patricia Priest who, quite appropriately, grew up in a Utah town called Bountiful (no, really). Even better than that though, the part of Lily Munster was played by the gorgeous Yvonne De Carlo, who I first fell for when I saw her dancing in the film *Salome*. I know *The Munsters* was considered to be a down-market version of *The Addams Family*, but with top class totty like Patricia and Yvonne, there really is no contest. I also have to admit to being partisan because, given their surname, I'm assuming the Munsters are third or fourth generation Irish. **WOL**

Question 67

Angela Rippon or
Anna Ford?

ANGELA RIPPON: The trailblazer; the first female prime-time newsreader. All others just followed in her wake, like seagulls trailing the QEII.

There was an unspoken U and Non-U differentiation going on between Angela and Anna. Angela might have been the BBC girl, with a voice that could dice diamonds, but we knew she was one of us. She was no bluestocking, despite having the legs for anything. Could you ever imagine Anna Ford strutting her stuff with Morecambe and Wise? No, because Anna would have a Concerned Women Against The Bomb meeting to go to.

Angela also has a life outside the news, contributing to such iconic shows as *Come Dancing* and the phenomenal *Masterteam*, in which her unforgettable pronunciation of "pot-pourri" transformed the attitude of a generation towards small bowls of desiccated flora. **FM**

ANNA FORD: Beautiful, sexy and intelligent; Ms Ford threw wine over Jonathan Aitken, inspired Reginald Bosanquet to write poetry and had a rose named after her. A winning hat trick, I believe. Anna didn't need to show us her legs. **CS**

Question 68

Roller skating or ice skating?

ROLLER SKATING: They are both ridiculous pursuits, and I have never mastered either, but at least with the roller variety you don't have to freeze your arse off while you're doing it. Being on four small wheels, as opposed to two thin blades, seems to me the best way to leave all your limbs - and some of your dignity - intact.

Then there's the problem of the vile boots. Skating means sharing one's footwear with hundreds, maybe even thousands, of others. There are enough germs in one, small boot to make a pathologist wince and the Hospital for Infectious Diseases clear its diary. This isn't fun; this is torture. Despite the brainwashing that goes on in films and television, it is not romantic to slide around on frozen water, wearing boots filled with bacteria. It is *dangerous*. Ice is for putting in drinks and it'll take more than Torville and Dean to convince me otherwise. **CS**

ICE SKATING: I've never gravely injured myself while ice skating, so I have rather a soft spot for it. Perhaps it's because ice skating tends to take place on a rink specifically designed for that very purpose and not in treacherous back gardens, inside large concrete tubes, or on the hard shoulder of the M62.

Ice skating is more sociable, too. Rather than screaming at you from passing cars, your fellow man is more likely to take pity on you and pick you up if you fall in his path. Everybody's there for the same reason – to have fun and maybe even flirt a bit. When you ice skate, it's always easy to pretend you're in a film. I'm usually in *Ice Follies of 1939*. **FM**

Question 69

Twiglets or Cheeselets?

TWIGLETS: How I loved these knobbly, Marmite-flavoured snacks. In fact, I was addicted to them, but my supply was irregular. My mum had decided to classify Twiglets as a treat rather than a staple, so we only got them very occasionally. I didn't get enough pocket money to keep buying them for myself, so what was I to do?

My younger brother saved me by suddenly developing a need to chew metal buckles. We found this out when Mum found the little idiot chewing away at a sandal, with blood trickling down his chin. To distract him, she bought him a sandal-shaped dog chew and this seemed to work. After that, she made sure he was never without a chew.

Noting the principle that had thus been established, I developed a compulsion to chew twigs. I made sure that I was seen doing it and a few days later, Mum came back from the shops with bags full of Twiglets. I was allowed to have a handful every time I felt the urge to chew twigs. This was an urge I felt with alarming regularity throughout my childhood. **WOL**

CHEESELETS: They are delicious and delightful. They are the perfect snack food: cheesy, but not too cheesy; crunchy, but not too… well, you get the picture. They make life better; they are gastronomic Prozac, but without the side effects (unless not being able to squeeze into a ra-ra skirt, because you've eaten too many of the damn things, can be counted as a side effect). How can bits of wood, smothered in a Marmite-like substance, compete? They can't. The only thing to be said in their favour is that only by rubbing a couple of Twiglets together did Ancient Man discover how to make fire. **CS**

Question 70

Action Man or the
Six Million Dollar Man?

ACTION MAN: My Action Man, Tommy, had eagle eyes (i.e. he could look left and right), gripping hands and realistic, cropped hair. He also had a range of weapons: hand pistols, grenades, rocket launchers and an armoured vehicle. He usually wore an outfit pretty similar to Edward Fox's in *A Bridge Too Far*, but he also had a frogman suit and an Argyll and Sutherland Highlanders' kilt outfit. He regularly slept with my sister's dolls, including the Lindsay Wagner 'Bionic Woman' doll, the Angie Dickinson 'Police Woman' doll and Donny and Marie Osmond (Donny was accidental and it was never spoken of again). In short, he was pretty damn cool and lived up to his name.

Now, given all that, how was I supposed to get excited about the Six Million Dollar Man action figure, which had painted on hair, red trainers and a red jogging outfit with a ridiculous, Elvis-style collar? Shame on all you kids who abandoned Action Man for this freak. **WOL**

THE SIX MILLION DOLLAR MAN: Action Girl was my favourite toy. The Emma Peel of the doll world. She was a tough chick and didn't mess about with any old action figure. She took one look at Action Man's gripping hand and eagle eye and wasn't impressed. Even when we gave a big, facial scar to the one who looked like Robert Shaw, she could pretty much take him or leave him. Things were looking dull in Doll World, when along came Steve.

He was gorgeous. His hair didn't feel like Astroturf and he didn't need a scar to look hard. He had a laser-sighted, bionic eye that you looked through to make everything seem far, far away. His bionic arm was amazing - you could peel back the elasticated skin to check out all his innermost circuits and he could lift huge weights with his lever-operated, bionic grip. Steve was invincible. In a fight, he'd have made Action Man cry for his mummy.

Action Girl liked Steve, but it didn't work out. When his TV show disappeared, so did he. So she ran off with a fully poseable Han Solo and never looked back. **FM**

Question 71

Rice Krispies or Puffa Puffa Rice?

RICE KRISPIES: Rice Krispies were one of two cereal types (the other was cornflakes) that provided the main ingredient in my mum's homemade cereal cup cakes.

Every other weekend of the summer holidays, I'd go camping with my friends. We'd all meet up and head towards the woods where we made a den. The den was a tent (an old bit of lino, thrown over a bush) in a small clearing, with a pit for making a campfire out of sticks and the tatty pages of an ancient porno-mag we'd found lying around.

We'd all be well supplied with butties, but I had something extra – a Tupperware box full of my mum's Krispie cakes. These chunks of Rice Krispies, mixed with toffee and covered in chocolate, were the biggest treat of summer and, because of them, I was the most popular member of our gang and got to be leader. Thanks, Mum. **WOL**

PUFFA PUFFA RICE: Well, exactly. To make Rice Krispies interesting, you have to cover them with caramel and chocolate. Puffa Puffa Rice never needed such superfluities and don't think that telling us cute stories about how you became Lord of the Flies can ever detract from that great truth.

Puffa Puffa Rice was undoubtedly the greatest of the rice-based cereals. I think it disappeared only because the world wasn't ready for its subtle, intoxicating, rich, brown sugar flavour. Who would have thought there could be such a world of difference between puffing and krisping a grain of rice? One grain becomes golden, smooth, sweet and scrumptious, the other turns into an edible wart-scab. Amazing.

The only thing wrong with Puffa Puffa Rice was that Sooty advertised it. But then again, who better to demonstrate the glories of this superb cereal than someone who has obviously become speechless with happiness at getting a free bowl? **FM**

Question 72

The Generation Game:
Bruce or Larry?

BRUCE FORSYTH: Bruce made *The Generation Game*. Everything anybody holds dear about it started with Brucie. He was King of the Catchphrase and even though Larry tried to make the show his own, "Shut that door!" - especially when there isn't a door - can never rival the likes of "Nice to see you, to see you, nice!" which always worked, even when it really wasn't.

Bruce made the stakes higher. If you were on Bruce's *Generation Game*, you not only had to beat the other contestants, make vases out of liquid jelly, read your panto lines off a performing dog, remember the teasmade *and* the yoghurt maker, lug home that damn cuddly toy and witness your dignity being kicked to a whimpering death in front of millions, you also had to survive the host. Like some prime-time Mephistopheles, he was forever hissing impossible instructions in your ear, chivvying you, doing his variety act while you struggled to stop your balloon animal exploding and mocking your very existence. If you won Bruce's *Generation Game*, you could call yourself a gladiator. **FM**

LARRY GRAYSON: He was the perfect host on the perfect game show. He was camp, sweet, genuinely funny and he didn't feel the need to patronise or intimidate the contestants. Indeed, he was usually more inept than they were. He dropped props, he forgot dance steps and appeared to be surrounded by chaos, but whether this was by design, or a happy accident, it worked. His sidekick, Isla, might not have won a lovely legs competition, but she could string a sentence together, carried off a strange, pudding-bowl hairstyle (something my sister, bless her, never managed in all her years at primary school) and was able to hold a tune. Anthea Redfern was too busy being blonde to do anything other than twirl, and Bruce was just a big, bossy chin on legs. He never seemed to like his contestants much and constantly rendered them all sweaty and helpless. The best thing about Bruce Forsyth is that he's not Jim Davidson. **CS**

Question 73

Plasticine or Play-Doh?

PLASTICINE: My younger brother was obsessed with trying to remodel used plasticine to look like fresh plasticine. He'd spend hours flattening it out to the right thickness, recreating the straight ridges on each piece, wrapping it back up in the cellophane, putting it back into the cardboard packaging and trying to fool people into thinking it was a new pack. The idiot.

Personally, I used to like making it into very soft little blocks. I would carry these around with me and secretly try to imprint people's car and house keys into them – just in case they ever held me hostage, or something.

There are so many uses for plasticine it would be impossible to list them all, but I understand that the 4th Tyldesley Scouts use plasticine to teach their boys how to plan the layout of a camp. As they themselves point out, this makes planning a campsite extremely non-boring. **WOL**

PLAY-DOH: Oh, the smell, the smell. God knows what it was, but I loved it. Then there were the colours (was hot pink ever hotter, or deep blue ever bluer?) and of course, the fabulous, tactile texture. I could spend all day just squeezing it through my fingers. Even now.

Play-Doh is a completely magical, sensory adventure. Squishing, sniffing, gazing, trying not to eat it because Mum said not to, but ooh, it looks so good…What's not to like? And what of the deep anguish you felt when you re-opened the pot after a long time and realised you'd let it dry out? That's why they invented counselling.

Plasticine is fine and dandy, but it'll never be the pleasure-overload that is Play-Doh. Plasticine's virtue lies in its usefulness and its superiority for modelling, as the 4th Tyldesley Scouts have correctly discovered and good for them. **FM**

Question 74

High Chaparral or Bonanza?

HIGH CHAPARRAL: *High Chaparral* seemed to be on television throughout the whole of the Seventies, and I, for one, thanked God for it. I'm sure my first words were "Big John". Born as I was in the Home Counties, where cattle rustling and fighting the Apache weren't exactly commonplace, *High Chaparral* was heady stuff. There was always so much going on; never a moment when a fight wasn't brewing, taking place or being resolved. I know it covered much the same ground as its predecessor, but it was done with oh, so much more flair. We had the beautiful Victoria, we had the even more beautiful Blue, and in the patriarch, Big John, we had a man who could have been hewn from the desert rocks themselves. *Bonanza* just didn't have the same glamorous appeal - how could it, with Hoss the Dross on board? It was the short, fat friend of a tall, willowy beauty. **CS**

BONANZA: It would be so easy to go with *High Chaparral* and that smouldering Argentinean minx, Linda Cristal, as the classy, but feisty, Victoria. She's certainly the ace card for *High Chaparral*, but while she was the main reason I liked watching it, she was also the main reason I found it almost unbearable. The very idea that someone so gorgeous could shack up with doddery, old Big John Cannon was anathema to a young man with fire in his loins.

Of course, as I've got older, I've had to get used to the idea that old men can somehow snare good-looking women. I'm sure that a few decades from now, I'll seek to invoke that very principle, but at the time it was all too much.

And in favour of *Bonanza*? Well, I liked the catchy theme tune, the straightforward, heroic simplicity and I especially liked the big lunk, Hoss. I wished I had a brother like that and lo, as time passed, I got one. **WOL**

Question 75

Musical Chairs or Pass the Parcel?

MUSICAL CHAIRS: I was not a competitive child, but injustice and unfairness got me really angry, especially if I was the victim and even more especially if it meant I was going to be cheated out of something – like the present being passed around in the parcel.

I noted very early on that the parent in control of the music for Pass the Parcel would inevitably favour the smallest child, the birthday child, or the blubbering child, all to the deliberate and malicious detriment of the larger, well-adjusted and well-behaved non-birthday children. That this unsporting behaviour was wielded so openly made matters even worse and I eventually refused to play unless an impartial referee was present.

Of course, Musical Chairs is also subject to the whims of unsporting judges, but plenty of training and practice (and cheating, which is always fine if the intention is to rectify an obvious injustice or lack of fair play by others,) could at least partially compensate for parental favouritism. There was actually a chance of winning.

I very much doubt that Pass the Parcel will ever be approved by the International Olympic Committee. **WOL**

PASS THE PARCEL: Oh my lord, Pass the Parcel - every time. Musical Chairs was just another name for an Under Nines gladiatorial contest. It was a licence for horrible boys and equally horrible girls to beat up those of us not built like aircraft hangers. I found Pass the Parcel to be a much more civilised way to pass the time. It gave me a chance to listen to the music and chat pleasantly to my neighbour. Even though we all knew the parents shamelessly rigged the games, nothing could mar my enjoyment of Pass the Parcel. Musical Chairs should be banned under the Human Rights Act. **CS**

Question 76

Chocolate teacakes or Wagon Wheels?

CHOCOLATE TEACAKES: This is a tale of two mallows: one soft and melt-in-your-mouth fluffy, the other claggy and chewy, sandwiched between two rounded chunks of stale-tasting biscuit.

Importantly, chocolate teacakes not only contain the right kind of marshmallow, they also contain the right amount. The Biscuit Research Institute of Krakow has a formula for gauging the optimum proportion of mallow to biscuit ($O = BM^5$). Chocolate teacakes match this formula precisely, whereas Wagon Wheels are almost an exact inversion of the formula. As if that weren't enough, can you really overlook the fact that teacakes also contain the added excitement of a small portion of jam underneath the mallow?

I fell in love with teacakes when I was a lad, as they would always make afternoon tea round at Nan's house so much more bearable. As I nodded along, feigning interest as the old dear wittered happily away, I couldn't help but notice the pleasing shape of these 'teasecakes', which often led me to ponder the joy of breasts. **WOL**

WAGON WHEELS: Are they smaller now, or did I get bigger? Never mind. They will always have a place in my heart. I once made myself sick by gorging on them and even that didn't put me off.

They're so satisfying and substantial; they're automatically more economical. One, single Wagon Wheel equals one, whole pack of teeny little chocolate teacakes. Those tiny-tot treats are mostly whipped air and the jam is no more than a decoy in a cynical bid for the hearts and minds of the Under Tens.

By the way, I heard the Biscuit Research Institute of Krakow was utterly discredited in the notorious "Jaffa: Cake or biscuit?" inquiry of 1992. **FM**

Question 77

Rupert or Pooh?

RUPERT: Everyone sing his name! I don't want to knock Pooh, but he's a bit of a stay-at-home, isn't he? He should have been on *Friends*, because all he ever does is hang out with his mates and have a "little something" now and again.

Rupert is a very different kind of bear. He has real adventures; genuinely amazing, fantastical, exotic adventures, with wonderfully weird, and sometimes quite disturbing, people and creatures. His world is totally magical and makes Pooh's look rather stockbroker-belt in comparison. Nutwood can be a very strange place – I remember being extremely unnerved by Raggety. But although he was frightening at first, he turned out all right in the end. That's the beauty of the *Rupert* books; nothing is ever quite as straightforward as it might appear. It can be as dark as it is captivating. And to top it all, he is Paul McCartney's favourite bear. **FM**

POOH: He understands the value of simplicity. He knows how to appreciate his surroundings, his friends, his honey and his hums. He shows us how to grow up and find contentment within ourselves, and in the minutiae of life. His "little somethings" are his great love and he doesn't let body image problems get in the way of enjoying them. Pooh never feels the need criticise the other animals, he just accepts them for what they are, foibles and all. The magic of the Hundred Acre Wood is gentler and less obvious than the flashy type found in Nutwood, but it's just as potent. Anyway, the scariest things in Nutwood are Rupert's monstrous, cat-sick yellow trousers. **CS**

Question 78

Screen Test or Clapperboard?

SCREEN TEST: Clapperboard was dull, dull, dull. When I got home from school, I didn't want to watch some old bloke interviewing some other old bloke about the intricacies of the blue-screen technique and how to add a laugh track to *Birth of a Nation*. No, I wanted to sit back, see some Disney clips and tell lovely Michael Rodd that the clock in the background was showing midnight and the biggest rhino was wearing *striped* shorts.

Plus, where else was I going to see all those Children's Film Foundation offerings? They certainly never came to a cinema near me, so this was my only chance. Mind you, they were never a patch on the Disney stuff; they always looked like out-takes from the *Double Deckers*. **FM**

CLAPPERBOARD: You may not appreciate the intricacies of the blue-screen technique, but I found it fascinating. Chris Kelly and *Clapperboard* revealed a lot about the supposedly glamorous world of films; mostly that it wasn't as glamorous as people supposed. Thanks to *Clapperboard*, I could sit in the cinema watching two films – the one on the screen and the one behind it. The hidden, technical side of film is often a hell of a lot more interesting than what you're supposed to be watching.

I admit that *Screen Test* was pretty good fun at first, a bit of welcome relief when you got home from a horrific double maths lesson, but after a while, the entertainment value began to wear thin. After all, the basic question of the programme was "Can kids pay attention long enough to absorb sixty seconds of visual information?" To which the answer was usually "No". Michael Rodd's improbably perfect hair was not enough in itself to compensate for the embarrassment. **WOL**

Question 79

Spirograph or Etch-a-sketch?

SPIROGRAPH: I always found this to be a very satisfying way to pass the time. There was something about spinning those plastic circles around that made me feel like a real artist.

Etch-a-sketch was definitely the inferior drawing tool, for many different reasons: the screen was too small for me to give my artistic impulse its true expression, I much prefer circles to straight lines and there was no finished product for me to keep and force my mother to stick on the fridge. **CS**

ETCH-A-SKETCH: Spirograph was only good for soppy circles, but Etch-a-sketch opened up the spectacular world of the quadrilateral. The great angled-shapes, squares and rectangles, were yours for the taking. It may have been a circle-free zone, but wavy lines were available to the more skilled practitioner. Why, it was a cornucopia of linear potential.

Etch-a-sketch was also ecologically sound. No waste paper with lots of circles on it, here.

And you could do that thing where you etched away at the same spot until you could see the mechanism working inside. Wow, it was fun. In fact, it was so much fun – and portable, too – I think the Question should be "Etch-a-sketch or laptop?" I know which I'd go for. **FM**

Question 80

Ready Brek or porridge?

READY BREK: It's child-friendly porridge. With the dour, lumpy stuff, there's always the fear that some sadist will serve it made with water and salt. This is never a possibility with Ready Brek; you're safely in milk-and-sugar world. The texture is finer and the taste is sweeter. Nothing bad is going to happen. Everything's going to be all right. And off you go to school; glowing like a light-sabre, ready to fight another day. **FM**

PORRIDGE: My dad always told me it puts hairs on your chest and increases your sperm count (salted porridge only). It's breakfast, for men. **WOL**

Question 81

Crazy golf or putting?

CRAZY GOLF: The best, most mindless, fun game in the world. Manically competitive types will always scorn crazy golf for the putting green, because they think putting guarantees a 'serious' win, but force them on to the crazy course and they have no choice but to surrender to the madness. Crazy golf isn't so much a game as a state of mind.

And talking of states, I honestly think crazy golf is the simplest route to world peace. Make the world leaders play a round together and see how they start getting along. If you win, it's great; but if you lose, well, what were your chances of getting the ball through the windmill's turning blades, up the pink elephant's bottom, around the scale model of St Paul's and into the clown's mouth, anyway? Let's go and have a choc-ice. **FM**

PUTTING: Putting is golf's version of speed dating. It's a cheaper, quicker, more direct, no-nonsense way to increase your chances of getting a hole-in-one whilst avoiding all the rough. **WOL**

Question 82

Top Cat or Deputy Dawg?

TOP CAT: Top Cat. He really was the most effectual Top Cat. And his intellectual, close friends were allowed to call him "T. C" – providing, of course, it was with dignity. Top Cat. He was, indisputably, the leader of the gang. He was the top, he was the tip, nay, I'd go so far as to say he was the championship. He was the most top, as well as the most tip, Top Cat. Yes, he was the chief, you might even say he was the king, but above everything, I'd like to remind everybody once again that he was the most tip top, Top Cat. **FM**

DEPUTY DAWG: Yes, ha ha, I get it. But *Top Cat* was an inferior, cartoon version of *Bilko* and therefore it was a copy rather than an original. Not so top, then.

Deputy Dawg stood for the moral right. His constant quest to keep the eggs in the hen house and the ice in the ice factory might not have been as exciting as the amoral hustling of Top Cat, but it had much more charm.

He also had the decency not to have an identity crisis. When reading through the television listings, I recall being promised *Boss Cat*, but when I tuned in, I was faced with a feline calling itself "Top". Make up your mind - are you Boss or Top? But that's cats for you. They won't commit to a name, or a day's hard graft.

Sometimes the good guy is best and Deputy Dawg, with his heart of gold, his drinker's nose and his distinctive southern drawl, is one of those cases. **CS**

Question 83

Space Invaders or Pacman?

SPACE INVADERS: This was the first video game I ever played and I still think it's the best. I like the fact that it fosters an ethic of self-sacrificing heroism. You take on the challenge of defending Earth from the Space Invaders, despite knowing beforehand that every wave you defeat is replaced by a quicker, faster-shooting wave; that there is a never ending supply of spaceships; they will not give up; and you will ultimately be destroyed. It's the kind of ending which appeals to my European sensibilities and I always felt that playing this game was a slightly more realistic experience than watching most Hollywood films, with their contractual-obligation, happy-ever-after finales.

As for Pacman, it was fine and fun in its way, but I think it soon became clear that there was limited enjoyment to be had from computer games based on normal daily experiences – such as eating, getting dressed, shaving, or going to the toilet. However, for most people, there are relatively few real-life opportunities to make destroying an alien mother ship your final, heroic act before bedtime. **WOL**

PACMAN: This game involved so much noshing, it was perfect for me. Pacman did nothing but eat. He ate the dots in the maze; he ate the power dot, so he could then eat the ghosts; and he ate the floating fruit when he'd eaten everything else.

Space Invaders was far too earnest, didn't involve snacking and was much harder to play. **CS**

Question 84

Cresta or Cream Soda?

CRESTA: I have extremely fond memories of Cresta. I know it came in different flavours, though I couldn't tell you what they were (probably toxaphene, riacin, cadmium and chlorinated paraffin), and the sensation you got while drinking it was pretty similar to accidentally swallowing a mouthful of pond-froth, but I loved it.

I don't know why Cresta isn't available any more, but I was told it was withdrawn from circulation after it was discovered that, due to the ingredients, possession of just one can created a breach of the Geneva Convention.

But if UN inspectors ever find a cache of it and they want it disposed of, they can certainly give me a call. I drank so much of it in the Seventies, I'm probably immune. **WOL**

CREAM SODA: You didn't have to chew before swallowing. **CS**

Question 85

The Famous Five or
The Hardy Boys?

THE FAMOUS FIVE: Read them all; loved them all. However, if I'm totally honest, it's the picnics that have stayed with me. All those lashings of ginger beer and plum cake might be a cliché, but whenever the *Famous Five* are mentioned, I start salivating.

I never bothered with *The Hardy Boys*. Why would I, when I had the adventures of Julian, Dick, George, Anne and Timmy to entertain me? Sandwiches aside, there were also islands, rowing boats, smugglers and treasure. *The Hardy Boys* were American and unnecessary. **CS**

THE HARDY BOYS: How embarrassing this comparison is for Britain. Whilst four English toffs and their dog were bicycling around Cornwall having problems getting on with some fairground folk, two American lads were off travelling the world in their quest to solve mysteries, smash crime rings and recover valuable stolen artefacts.

I admit that when it comes to rescuing kidnapped scientists, the Famous Five were right up there with Joe and Frank Hardy. I also accept that the Boys had their fair share of *Famous Five*-type 'upper-class' crimes to solve, like the theft of a collection of silk moths, or a missing chess trophy. But in their time, the Hardy Boys have also foiled a terrorist plan to create havoc in America, recovered stolen radioactive isotopes and foiled a plot to build an atomic weapon. You could bet that the Hardy Boys would have discovered Weapons of Mass Destruction in Iraq, if there had been any. Meanwhile, the Famous Five would have been faffing about, solving the Mystery of the Flat Ginger Beer and being terribly condescending to Nobby, the circus boy and Pongo, the chimp. **WOL**

Question 86

Dodgems or waltzer?

DODGEMS: I became aware of the social function of dodgems at the age of seven.

The first time I sat behind the wheel of a dodgem car, I assumed that the objective of the ride was to dodge oncoming vehicles, so I spent several minutes carefully avoiding all the other cars before my dad jumped in, pushed me to one side in exasperation and took control. With great satisfaction, he made sure we hit every other dodgem at maximum speed. Now an idle passenger, I looked around and saw that I was not alone – in every car there was a confused looking kid with a manic father at the wheel. I suddenly understood what it was all about and since then, I've noted that the incidence of road rage has increased in direct proportion to the decline of this hugely significant ride. **WOL**

WALTZER: No fairground ride will ever come close to the waltzer. The thrill of being hurled around in those ridiculous round things simply can't be matched. Never have I screamed louder, or laughed harder, than in one of those saucers-from-hell. And I will never forget the image of my father attempting to light his pipe while in mid-flight.

The dodgems were to be avoided at all costs - partly because you had to drive yourself, but mainly because it meant being constantly rammed by psychopaths. **CS**

Question 87

James Hunt or Niki Lauda?

HUNT: Hunt the Shunt was the perfect Formula One racing driver. A Grand Prix winner who made manifest the devil-may-care creed of the time. When he turned up at the track, you had no doubt that he'd just left the arms of some leggy Swedish model, whose name he couldn't remember and whose telephone number he'd already lost. Quite an achievement for a man born in Belmont, Surrey.

Hunt had naff blond hair, some worrying jewellery, smoked fags while he drove and drank like a fish. This should have been reprehensible, but it wasn't; it was exciting. Lauda was courageous, smart and talented, so why he seems dull by comparison is beyond me. **CS**

LAUDA: Niki Lauda won the Formula One championship three times: 1975, 1977 and 1984. The last two were most remarkable for the fact that he had died on the operating table following a crash in 1976. That's real commitment. **WOL**

Question 88

Eurovision: Brotherhood of Man or Buck's Fizz?

BROTHERHOOD OF MAN: They didn't have to rely on tearing women's clothes off to get attention. They won Eurovision fair and square, thanks to a quirky little dance that was the rage of the playground and the most charming song ever written about the dark side of babysitting. And it was quite a coup to get Des Lynam on lead vocals.

Buck's Fizz were a mystery to me. Mike looked like he should have been called Bobby and Bobby looked very much like a Mike. Jay looked like she wished she wasn't there and Cheryl wore a permanent grin of shocked glee, like someone about to be hit by an ice cream van. At least Brotherhood of Man never let anybody know their names and for that alone, I give them douze points. **FM**

BUCK'S FIZZ: They had bright costumes, leaped about, ripped skirts off and sang a much better song. Brotherhood of Man seemed so much older and more staid. They had an earnest name and they wore suits and bobble hats. *Save All Your Kisses for Me* was hellish to dance to and even the group seemed flummoxed. Head waggling and a strange foot shuffle is not a quirky dance routine, it's a twitch. **CS**

Question 89

Film chases:
French Connection or
Bullitt?

THE FRENCH CONNECTION: Both car chases are the perfect reflection of the films themselves, so if you prefer yours flashy and artificial, then *Bullitt* would be for you. If, however, you like your films (and chases) hard boiled, dark, dogged and visceral, then, like me, you'd go for *The French Connection*. There are no hip Mustangs, or sunny surroundings, to distract us from the mayhem and madness. *The French Connection* uses much darker, seedier locations, which lend the proceedings a claustrophobic feel that is further enhanced by the fact that the director, William Friedkin, insisted on it being shot in one take and some of the hair-raising 'stunts' are for real. All this makes us feel like we are actually in that car with Popeye Doyle, and we ain't coming out 'til the bad guy's caught. Now that's what I call a car chase. **CS**

BULLITT: Admit it. When you think of the ultimate movie car chase, you think of *Bullitt*, don't you? It's the slickest, most stylish example of a couple of boy-racers smashing the hell out of their suspensions in the history of film.

I imagine the conversation in the *French Connection* production office went something like this: "Hey, let's have a car chase!" "Nah, we couldn't do it better than *Bullitt* – we need a new angle. How about they chase a boat? Or a plane?" "Ooh! Ooh! I know! They could chase a train!" So they do. But without an ounce of Frank Bullitt's panache.

The *Bullitt* chase has such a satisfying end, too – a nice, big conflagration engulfing the bad guys, as Frank speeds away. In fact, the only flaw is that his insipid, whiny girlfriend isn't in the other car when it explodes. **FM**

Question 90

Vimto or
Dandelion and Burdock?

VIMTO: The smell of the summer of 1975, in a can. Or a bottle, if you can remember that far back. Oh, the fruity, dark red fabness of it all. Watching it being poured out and running out to play, carrying a big glassful. Then dropping it and watching it soak into the grass. Heaven.

It was the North's answer to Coke. Come to think of it, Vimto is the North's answer to pretty much everything. Dandelion and Burdock is a good, traditional drink and never to be scorned, but in the battle of the British dark drinks, I think its sharpness loses out to Vimto's blackcurrant-laden sweetness. My Auntie Pat loves it, though. **FM**

DANDELION AND BURDOCK: When I was a child, this was the perfect drink with the perfect name. It said picnics, it said gingham clothes, it said wholesomeness, it said perfection. Those of us growing up in the Seventies must have had stomachs capable of safely housing nuclear waste, as there is no other way we could have survived the surfeit of sugar and chemical detritus we poured down our necks, but Dandelion and Burdock was different from the other drinks. It was made from nourishing herbs and because my mother said it was good for me, I could drink it as I would water in a desert. It was liquid heaven. It was, quite simply, the best. **CS**

Question 91

The Water Margin or Monkey?

THE WATER MARGIN: Ah, the magic of the Orient. Inscrutability, improbable leaping, infallible swordsmanship and slender-hipped, dark-haired, athletic women came pouring into my living room, and my consciousness, for two, wondrous years.

I was totally transfixed by this series, which profoundly impacted on my youth. I began to take a deep interest in Chinese history, I took karate classes, I bought David Sylvian albums and I started fancying oriental women.

The fascination with oriental women lasted substantially longer than my interest in Chinese history (there's too much of it), even though *The Water Margin* served to caution against expecting any long lasting relationships, because the heroines tended to die with alarming regularity.

As for karate, I gave it up when I realised I'd never be able to leap fifty feet into the air, or whip the head off the school bully with my toes. (I made it to Sixth Kyu, a green belt, which means I can twist the tops off difficult jars.) I don't want to talk about David Sylvian. **WOL**

MONKEY: *Monkey* was a sort of Japanese pantomime version of *The Wizard of Oz*, with a nod to *Star Trek* along the way. Weird TV doesn't come much weirder than this, so you have to love it.

The mad monkey, the pig-demon and the magic, fish-type bloke all helped the Buddha to get to India and find the sacred scriptures - except they didn't, because the series was cancelled. So all I can do is recall the glory days of what would now be called *Crouching Monkey, Hidden Pig* and bemoan the loss of Monkey's pet pink cloud that came when he called, the bizarre dubbing, the school-play sets and the one series that didn't take kung-fu at all seriously. *The Water Margin* was way too solemn for its own good and could have done with a monkey whose staff could grow to any length, or who talked in tongues whenever his ring tightened. Well, wouldn't we all. **FM**

Question 92

Frisbee or ball?

FRISBEE: There is something very lame about just throwing a ball about. It needs to be hit, kicked, or putted, for it to seem anything other than a complete waste of time. The Frisbee, on the other hand, is made for no other purpose than to be thrown. It wasn't ever meant to be part of a game; it's the game itself. Playing with a Frisbee makes leaping about in the fresh air an almost enjoyable experience. Who'd have thought it? **CS**

BALL: Ball games: Shinty; hurling; football; rugby; hockey; lacrosse; baseball; basketball; volleyball; tennis; squash; ping-pong; cricket; softball; petanque, golf, etc.
Frisbee games: Er…Frisbee.
I think Frisbee came about because some people have severe visual-spatial problems and are unable to catch spherical objects, even if thrown straight to them at extremely low velocities. The Frisbee ensures that they can play throw and catch (with a larger, slower object) like normal people and so don't feel so conspicuous, even though they usually wear Hawaiian shirts. **WOL**

Question 93

Spot the difference: Michael York or Simon MacCorkindale?

MICHAEL YORK: I saw *Riddle of the Sands* twice before I realised these two weren't the same person. It has to be said that neither of them set my pants on fire, but at least Michael didn't star in *Manimal*, was able to keep control of his nostrils and had the grace to make one cult film.

Simon MacCorkindale looks too much like a big, public schoolboy. If he had played D'Artagnan, it would have been in cricket whites. I would challenge anyone to name five famous programmes or films in which he starred and stay awake while they were doing it. **CS**

SIMON MacCORKINDALE: *Manimal*; *Jesus of Nazareth*; *Manimal*; *I, Claudius*; *Manimal*...I'm still awake...*Death on the Nile* and *Falcon Crest*...Shall I go on?

I realise that these two floppy-haired, upper-class British actors can be difficult to tell apart, so I'll point out one foolproof method: Simon's nose is at right angles to his face. **FM**

Question 94

The Waltons or Little House on the Prairie?

THE WALTONS: Firstly, the best theme tune. Secondly, a woman called Michael (how often does that happen?) and thirdly, the loveliest family since the Osmonds, but with extra girls.

Little House was deeply confusing. Nobody ever changed their clothes, children appeared out of nowhere, disappeared, went blind, everybody was called Melissa – it made my head spin. By contrast, the Waltons were a reliable, comforting presence and even though they were struggling through the Depression, you never saw them eat squirrel and their goodnight chorus was inspirational. God bless.

The Waltons also came up with the excellent idea of suffixing a child's name with its gender - John *Boy* - so nobody could get confused. How come that never caught on?

But most importantly, the Waltons had a whole mountain named after them. Their very own mountain! How could the uninspired Ingalls, who had the whole of North America to choose from and yet still settled on the flattest, dullest stretch of field imaginable, beat that? **FM**

LITTLE HOUSE ON THE PRAIRIE: *Little House on the Prairie* was all about goodness in wooden huts. It was soft-focus frontier life, which is how I like it; everything was clean and nothing was killed. There was no problem that Ma and Pa Ingalls couldn't solve with a few homilies and some vigorous ploughing. With his sturdy braces and timeless hair, Charles led his family through all the trials and tribulations Walnut Grove could throw at them. Yet even when Nellie Olsen did her worst, I was never in any doubt that good would prevail and love would win the day.

The Waltons were just too odd to be comforting. Stuck on that mountain, wearing those dungarees, not seeing many folks from outside those parts, all looking horribly similar…Oh dear. **CS**

Question 95

First aftershave:
Old Spice or Brut?

OLD SPICE: I have to champion this because it smells so good. Believe it or not, I've never used aftershave, but I must admit that I'm partial to an Old Spice kinda guy. It says manly, it says fresh, it says bronzed hunks surfing epic waves as the *Carmina Burana* blasts forth. It doesn't say Henry Cooper after a laddish tussle in the locker room with Kevin Keegan. **FM**

BRUT: I got my first aftershave at the age of 15, about one-and-a-half years before I actually started shaving, and it was Brut. Perhaps the time that lapsed between receiving it and using it didn't help, but it was like pouring vinegar into an open wound.

At first I wanted to defect to Denim, because its adverts suggested that rapid chest hair growth would follow and cheap women would find themselves compelled to undo your shirt and rub you. But I persevered with Brut, especially once it became apparent that using it was a badge of honour. Not only were you man enough to lacerate your face with cold steel, but you also heroically splashed your scars with a substance that felt like it was only one grade lower than Agent Orange on the dangerous chemicals index.

At the age of eighteen I gave up shaving altogether and started growing a beard. Although I considered Denim, and aspired to Old Spice, I never actually used anything other than Brut. **WOL**

Question 96

Mary Poppins or Bedknobs and Broomsticks?

MARY POPPINS: How Dick Van Dyke didn't get so much as an Oscar nomination for his acutely observed, singing Cockney chimneysweep is one of the greatest mysteries in the history of cinema. Unbelievably, he wasn't even the best thing about this film. You can't go wrong with Julie Andrews and it's her presence that makes *Mary Poppins* infinitely more watchable than *Bedknobs*. (That, and the fact I have an irrational and deeply felt aversion to Angela Lansbury.)

What is it about Julie Andrews that makes her so engaging to old and young alike? As a child, I just knew that if I were ever to have a nanny, I would want it to be the firm but fair, fun and fey Mary Poppins. Later, as a teenager awash with manly feelings, I contemplated the possibility that under that prim and proper exterior there was an insatiable tigress, barely contained within that tight, Edwardian corset. So, it's a big yes to *Mary Poppins* and an even bigger YES to Julie Andrews. **WOL**

BEDKNOBS AND BROOMSTICKS: The first film I saw twice. No childhood is complete without a full appreciation of flying beds, animatronic armour and soccer playing hippos. It's an enchanting, entrancing experience and my favourite Disney film ever. Bless you, Walt. Bless you.

Mary Poppins just tortures me with notions of what housework could be like if I could fly, talk to animals and had a really big handbag. Admittedly, it also took the mixing of live-action and animation to new heights, but *Bedknobs* ultimately takes that prize too, for honing the technique to perfection.

Both films have the great David Tomlinson – hooray! But in *Bedknobs*, he's not cancelled out by Dick Van Dyke – hip, hip, hooray! Anyway, Eglantine saves Britain from the Nazi threat, whereas Mary just tidies up a bit then flies off into the sunset. Give me the war-heroine every time. **FM**

Question 97

Subbuteo or Scalextric?

SUBBUTEO: For those young boys whose finger control was more finely honed than their feet, this was the only way to play football. Also, you didn't have to play in the rain, suffer the embarrassment of being picked next to last (poor fatty Simon Hardacre was always last), or take group showers afterwards. Just go around to your friend's house with a supply of crisps and biscuits, roll out the pitch and get flicking.

I never experienced the joy of actually owning Subbuteo, as my dad refused to buy it until they made a set of players in the Colby F.C. strip. One Christmas, in the mid-Seventies, I thought he had relented. I could hardly contain my excitement as I tore off the wrapping paper, but couldn't contain my disappointment when I saw the word on the box was not Subbuteo, but Scalextric. We spent a miserable afternoon watching the cars fly off every bend on the unimaginative figure-of-eight track, packed the thing away on Boxing Day and donated it to Oxfam a few months later.

I can barely describe how rubbish Scalextric was compared to Subbuteo, but I recently went back to that same Oxfam shop to buy some vests, and the Scalextric set was still there, unwanted, twenty-seven years later. **WOL**

SCALEXTRIC: It wasn't always easy to assemble and had the life span of a mayfly, but for the brief millisecond it worked, Scalextric let me kiss joy's coattails. Driving those cars round that figure of eight (oh yes, no boring oval track layout for me) was about the most exciting thing to happen since the rather spectacular explosion of my Clackers. Flicking a badly painted bit of plastic around a mangy piece of green felt simply could not compare with being the first female Formula One racing driver in the world. **CS**

Question 98

Space 1999 or
Battlestar Galactica?

SPACE 1999: As a lad, I'd have punched anyone who said I fancied an alien metamorph with beaded eyebrows and big, brown sideburns. But in *Space 1999*, Catherine Schell taught me to be more open-minded about such things. When it first started, her character, Maya, along with those cool Eagle landing craft, made me wonder if my future career lay in space travel.

After a while, I realised this might not be such a good idea. Space was proving to be a very dangerous place. Cries of "The Eagle has landed!" were heard rather less often than "The Eagle has crashed!" The constant exploding of these so-called 'landing' craft was the main cause of death on Moonbase Alpha. Even if you avoided that, there was always the possibility of being crushed by alien brain antibodies, or something equally horrible. At the end of another episode, the realisation that Captain Koenig would have to write a letter beginning "Dear Mr and Mrs Mateo, I regret to inform you that your son has tragically been killed by his own ghost during an exorcism" was enough to make me abandon the idea of joining the space programme. That is, until the end of series two, when Blake Maine's cause of death was recorded as "killed by alien dominatrices". Yep, I was back on board. **WOL**

BATTLESTAR GALACTICA: Just let me get this straight. Did *Space 1999* have Dirk Benedict, leaping around in tight, tight jodhpurs, flicking his fabulous hair out of his sparkling eyes and making my heart leap every time he heroically blasted yet another evil Cylon away to the great scrapyard in the sky? No, I didn't think it did. So remind me, why are we having this conversation? **FM**

Question 99

Conkers or Clackers?

CONKERS: Conkers has a long tradition as a favourite game of urchins and working class kids. With the horse chestnuts falling in September and October, it was an ideal start-of-the-school-year game in workhouses and comprehensives, as the essential materials were free. As kids in posh schools were all busy selecting their start of term 'fags' and playing rugger, we'd be out trying to find a potential champion conker and nicking the string from the waistbands of sleeping tramps.

I long harboured a dream of becoming the school champion, making everyone call me William the Conkerer and perhaps winning a conker scholarship to some half-decent grammar school. But it was not to be. I was stuck in comprehensives throughout my education.

As a result, I would always be sure to gather up the broken pieces of defeated conkers, because extract of horse chestnut can be used to treat malaria, diarrhoea, frostbite and ringworm, all of which were prevalent throughout the autumn and winter terms. **WOL**

CLACKERS: Clackers were a magnificent invention. Few things before, or since, have given me such satisfaction as handling a pair of Whackers. I'm sure they're the balls of the devil, but I loved them. They were loud enough to be heard in space, drove my parents to threaten adoption and were (so myth had it) based on a South American hunting weapon. Hurrah!

Conkers were too tame, too *Just William* and far, far too quiet. **CS**

Question 100

Butch or Sundance?

BUTCH: Many people might think this is the "Paul Newman or Robert Redford?" Question, but that would include discussions about their other films and salad dressing, etc. This Question is all about *that* film and how cool the characters are.

Butch never blew a man's brains out and that alone makes him the outlaw for me. He was the perfect cocktail of sweetness, wit, intelligence and world-weary cynicism. He was, in short, delicious. I think he's so sexy and I can't understand why the schoolmarm didn't run away with him. They should have ridden off into the sunset together, on his bicycle.

Of course, it helps that 'Butch Cassidy' sounds slightly less like a gay nightclub than 'the Sundance Kid' and Butch didn't grow a camp, bouffant moustache that would have been fine in downtown San Francisco, but was less appropriate in the Wild West. **CS**

SUNDANCE: For me, the Sundance Kid wins it, even though his real name was Harry Longabaugh. He was the toughest, the brightest and the coolest. Unlike Butch, he actually killed people, which is the whole point of being an outlaw. He got the great corduroy jacket; he got the bad-guy black hat; he got the girl. Butch, on the other hand, had to wear a bowler hat and ride around on a bicycle, while someone crooned *Raindrops Keep Fallin' On My Head*. In that one scene, he falls so far behind on the cool-o-meter that there isn't enough time left to claw back the points.

I know someone called Butch and he has a moustache (no, he's straight). This confused me for a while, because in the film, Sundance has a moustache and Butch doesn't. But Sundance is still the right answer. **WOL**

Question 101

Meltis New Berry Fruits or The Apocalypse?

MELTIS NEW BERRY FRUITS: The really great thing about Meltis Fruits, with their weird combination of jelly, crunchiness and unexpected, liquid centre, was that very few people actually liked them. They were a vamped-up, English version of the superior, European fruit *pastille* and, maybe because they were so overwhelmingly sugary, they were perfect for Christmas.

In fact, Granny was the only person who fought with me to get them. After a few years of losing to her at arm wrestling, my strategy - from Christmas Day 1979 - was to keep plying her with sherry until she fell asleep in the middle of *Doctor Zhivago*. Then I'd retire to the kitchen with the box and stuff myself until I was sick.

They were the ideal Christmas present, because almost everyone you gave them to took one bite and handed them straight back. **WOL**

THE APOCALYPSE: Oh, the excitement of that first-ever box of New Berry Fruits. The jewel-bright colours; the tempting, sugar coating; the scrumptious promise of jelly-heaven. Then, the first bite. I'll never forget that liquid middle, tasting like the worst mumps medicine ever, and the deep, desolate disappointment that followed.

Then came the anger. How could anything that looked so good taste so bad? Why play such a cruel trick on helpless children? In the name of confectionery, why?

After that experience, I feel like I've pretty much experienced the Apocalypse already. I've known disillusion, frustration and betrayal. I've had the candy taken from me. If it's a choice between a possible brush with Death, Slaughter, Famine and War, or definitely having to eat another New Berry Fruit, I'll take my chances with the guys.

So come on, you horsemen, if you think you're hard enough; do your worst. In fact, I challenge you all to try a New Berry Fruit. Whoever screams first gets a big box for Christmas. **FM**

If you've enjoyed The Retro Questions and fancy joining
in the discussion, visit

www.thequestions.co.uk

Question 102

The Questions books:
Classic or Retro?

CLASSIC: The original and best. The Retro Questions are undeniably entertaining, but they're still the spin-off, the junior partner. With the Classic Questions, you're getting the daddy of them all.

I like their inclusiveness, too. The Retros can be like an exclusive club, which can have a down-side; ask a callow youth whether they prefer Bodie to Doyle and they'll look at you like you probably remember banana rationing. But you can ask anybody a Classic Question, anybody at all. I'm especially keen to ask the chairman of McVities: "Jaffa: cake or biscuit?"

The Classic Questions are your official, laminated, access-all-areas pass to the wonderful world of The Questions and the best bit is, they'll never make you feel old. **FM**

RETRO: The Retro Questions are an easier option than the Classics. Deciding if *Blue Peter* is better than *Magpie* doesn't require so much energy as finding out if you've just met a Roundhead or a Cavalier, or coping with the sort of wild passions that "The Beatles or the Stones?" arouses.

The Retros are for birthday parties, or any party come to that; they can be used to cheer people up, or boost morale. They are also a good way to work out someone's age, if they're reluctant to divulge it, and can be less intimidating for those new to the concept of the Questions. The Classic Questions have their place, to be sure, but it's the Retro Questions that will bring out the party poppers, the Jammie Dodgers and the best in people. **CS**

Fiona McCade: *Having destroyed her good twin in the womb, Fiona is an only child. She spent her formative years trying to turn her parents' garage into the National Theatre of Yorkshire, so nobody was surprised when she went on to be a professional actress. This led to some theatre work, occasional film and TV parts and a great deal of temping.*
While playing Emma Peel she got a nasty case of leather-burn, so she became a freelance writer, broadcaster and columnist for The Scotsman. *She currently lives in Edinburgh with a tame Manxman and a large collection of Napoleonic literature.*
Fiona's greatest regret is that she didn't grow up to be Daphne from Scooby-Doo.

William O' Leary *was raised in Yorkshire and the Isle of Man. Before university he travelled to North America where, in 1984, he helped Courtney Cox onto the stage during the filming of Bruce Springsteen's* Dancing in the Dark *video.*
Following higher education, he worked for the Carpathian Forestry Board before settling in New Zealand for five years where he found employment as a fireman, carpenter and artist's model. Returning to the UK to establish a moorhen sanctuary in Cumbria, William continues to eke out a living from fees received for his appearance in a series of Australian toilet roll commercials.
William once broke both legs jumping out of his bedroom window on a Space Hopper.

Cath Sutton: *Cath was born in Surrey and is the middle sister of three, although she's never longed to visit Moscow. However, before and during studying at Manchester University she did travel to New Zealand, India and throughout Europe. Despite being a pogo stick prodigy and exhibiting a startling aptitude for this highly-skilled discipline throughout her childhood, she decided not to pursue it as a career and became a counsellor for a women's health organisation instead.*
Cath never won a Blue Peter *badge, but ate enough Space Dust to give herself a rash.*